The Singing Spirit

Volume 18

SUN TRACKS

An American Indian Literary Series

Series Editor

Larry Evers

Editorial Committee

Vine Deloria, Jr.   Emory Sekaquaptewa

N. Scott Momaday   Leslie Marmon Silko

Joy Harjo   Ofelia Zepeda

The Singing Spirit

EARLY SHORT STORIES BY

NORTH AMERICAN INDIANS

EDITED BY BERND C. PEYER

THE UNIVERSITY OF ARIZONA PRESS

TUCSON & LONDON

THE UNIVERSITY OF ARIZONA PRESS

Copyright © 1989
The Arizona Board of Regents
All Rights Reserved

This book was set in 10/13 Ehrhardt.
Manufactured in the United States of America
⊗ This book is printed on acid-free, archival-quality paper.

93   3

Library of Congress Cataloging-in-Publication Data
The Singing spirit : early short stories by North American Indians /
edited by Bernd C. Peyer.
p.   cm. — (Sun tracks : an American Indian literary series ;
v. 18)
Bibliography: p.
Cloth ISBN 0-8165-1114-4 (alk. paper)
Paper ISBN 0-8165-1220-5 (alk. paper)
1. Short stories, American—Indian authors.   2. Indians of North
America—Fiction.   3. American fiction—20th century.   4. American
fiction—19th century.   I. Peyer, Bernd.   II. Series: Sun tracks ;
v. 18.
PS508.I5S56   1989   89-32419
813'.01083520397—dc20   CIP
British Cataloguing-in-Publication Data
A catalogue record for this book is available from the British Library.

Contents

Realization of this anthology was made possible by a Ford Foundation Fellowship to the D'Arcy McNickle Center for the History of the American Indian, Newberry Library. I am deeply grateful to the wonderful staff at the center and that venerable storage bank of knowledge. I would also like to thank those who helped me trace some of the stories included here: Larry Evers, Birgit Hans, Peter Nabokov, Dorothy Parker, LaVonne Ruoff-Brown, and Terry Wilson.

Introduction

Recent scholarship has provided new insights into the subject of early American Indian literature.[1] Nevertheless, works written by Indians prior to World War II remain relatively inaccessible. They were often published by small, transient presses or journals, and references to them are scarce. The purpose of this anthology is to introduce some of the major Indian authors of the late nineteenth and early twentieth centuries by way of one of the more elusive genres in the history of Indian writing: the short story. The focus here will be on fictional stories and not on the more numerous transcriptions of orally transmitted legendary tales.[2]

Creative writing played only a small role in Indian literature until the later 1960s. Indian authors of past generations generally functioned as "informants" and, as in the case of slave-narrative writers, sought to render their experiences objectively. Ethnographic data —the more superficial details of daily Indian life—seems to have been easier to market than human attributes like the imagination. A sense of authenticity was and still is a primary criterion for the acceptability of Indian literature. The belles lettres are held to be one of civilization's ultimate achievements, while at the same time they frequently portray Indian life as civilization's antithesis, or at best its infant stage. Consequently, the bulk of early Indian writings is expository, and touches of the "informant" permeate the first attempts at fiction.

With the above in mind, I have been somewhat flexible in my choice of stories and have included autobiographical as well as satirical sketches that may not stand up to an overly strict definition of fiction. Furthermore, as this is intended to be a book by Indians about Indians, the selection is limited to stories with Indian themes, thus omitting possible inclusions by Will Rogers, Lynn Riggs, and others.

From its inception in 1772 with the publication of Samson Occom's *A Sermon, Preached at the Execution of Moses Paul, an Indian* until the close of the Civil War, Indian literacy was almost exclusively the offspring of missionary activity.[3] The Methodists and Presbyterians in particular were instrumental in the development of early Indian literature during two periods of evangelical fervor recorded in history as the Great Awakening (c. 1730–1750) and the Second Great Awakening (c. 1800–1840). Outstanding literary figures such as Samson Occom (1723–1792), William Apes (1798–1839), George Copway (1818–1869), and Peter Jones (1802–1856) were Methodist or Presbyterian clergymen. Others, like the Cherokee journalist Elias Boudinot (1804–1839), were not ordained but were in the employ of missionary societies. Their liturgical writings (sermons, conversion testimonies, missionary journals) thus closely reflect the attitudes of their mentors, who tended to view the imagination with some suspicion and expected literature to fulfill a moral purpose. Salvation of the soul dominated as a theme until Indian removal was undertaken in earnest in the 1820s and, as Roy Harvey Pearce pointed out, a more diverse interest slowly developed among writers and publishers in search of an American heritage.[4] Autobiographies—notably those describing an individual Indian's progress from "the deep woods to civilization"—and tribal histories appear in increasing numbers during the nineteenth century, frequently combined in a single monograph. At this time David Cusick (d. 1840) also transcribed tribal legends and published them in his *Sketches of the Ancient History of the Six Nations* (1827), and George Copway later adapted several traditional tales to the short-story format in *The Traditional History and Characteristic Sketches of the Ojibway Nation* (1850; these were also reprinted in his short-lived weekly, *Copway's American Indian*, in 1851).[5]

Only two antebellum examples of Indian fiction have yet come to light: Elias Boudinot's rather dubious *Poor Sarah* (1823) and John R. Ridge's *The Life and Adventures of Joaquin Murieta* (1854). The former, however, is a typical religious character sketch that had already appeared anonymously in a Boston newspaper in 1820, when Boudinot was still attending mission school. It is thus quite probable that he merely reprinted it at the Cherokee press in line with his own duties as a missionary. If so, Ridge's imaginary biography of the famous California bandit, which is obviously patterned after Sir Walter Scott's romances, would be the first work of fiction actually written by an Indian, albeit without an Indian theme.[6]

Indian fiction does not appear again until the end of the nineteenth century, following major shifts in Indian-white relations as well as publishing history. The decades between 1870 and 1920 wrought drastic changes among North America's Indians. They marked the end of tribal autonomy and the completion of the confinement to reservations of all Indian groups within U.S. territory. The consequent Indian dependence on the federal government, in turn, made new Indian policies necessary, especially since segregation by removal to unwanted areas was no longer feasible.

Debate over a new Indian policy was triggered by the famous Ponca case in 1879, which became the cause célèbre around which eastern philanthropists and clergymen could rally as "friends of the Indian." The attempt by a group of Ponca under the leadership of Luther Standing Bear (not to be confused with the Sioux author of the same name) to return to their tribal lands after having been forcefully removed found great public sympathy and led to the founding of organizations like the Indian Rights Association (founded in 1882), the Women's National Indian Association (founded in 1883), and the National Indian Defense Association (founded in 1885) for the purpose of solving the perennial "Indian problem." It was generally agreed that Indians would have to adopt Anglo-American ways or face extinction. The introduction of private property and improvements in education were to bring about this transformation, which became the purported goal of the General Allotment Act (the Dawes Act) of 1887.

The latter part of the 1870s is also often viewed as a turning point in Indian education because from that point on the federal government progressively increased its involvement in that sector. Congressional appropriations increased twentyfold so that by 1895 some two hundred institutions were providing services to approximately eighteen thousand students.[7] Although still concerned with the teaching of Christian principles, these schools followed the more temporal guidelines set by the Hampton Institute, a vocational training school for Black freedmen that in 1878 had opened its doors to Indian students as well. It sought to teach its charges farming and other secular occupations rather than to prepare them for the pulpit or for missionary activities. Besides dramatically increasing the number of Indian students (and possible authors), this new educational policy inevitably created a class of Indian professionals who cooperated with the reformers. Since a substantial number of students were recruited from the more recently subdued Plains tribes, the dominance that eastern Indians had established in letters and the professions quickly diminished.

The turn of the century thus witnessed what could be called the rise of an Indian intellectual elite, which greatly enriched literary production. Many were among the founding or active members of the Society of American Indians (SAI), the first national Indian political organization, established in 1911. Its platform coincided with the policies of the Dawes Act, which favored private allotment of tribal lands, individual citizenship (granted collectively in 1924), and improved educational and vocational services. Points of view differed, however, concerning such key issues as whether to support the continuation of reservations or the Bureau of Indian Affairs, and such disputes finally led to the disbanding of the organization in the mid-1920s. Members left behind a substantial body of writings in the SAI's *Quarterly Journal* (later renamed *American Indian Magazine*) as well as numerous publications in major national magazines. Another forum for Indian writers of this era was provided by the various Indian-school publications, including *The Southern Workman*, from the Hampton Institute; *The Indian Leader* (Haskell Institute), *The Red Man* (Carlisle Indian School), and *The Indian School Journal* (Chilocco Boarding School).[8]

The sheer number of publications and the variety of genres indicate that Indian literature experienced an unprecedented boom at the turn of the century. Although the reformers' zeal waned considerably after the enactment of the Dawes Act, their public efforts and publications such as Helen Hunt Jackson's *A Century of Dis-*

honor (1881) and *Ramona* (1884) continued to generate an interest in Indians. This was enhanced by the mass publishing industry, which, beginning in the 1840s, vastly increased the market for literature as a whole. Of special significance for the development of Indian fiction was the emergence of national magazines that could reach millions of readers. They not only popularized the short story but also elevated it to a bona fide genre in literature.

Postbellum America also underwent a phase of nationalistic fervor that precipitated a search by its intellectuals for a truly unique American identity. The contemporary literati, in their effort to distinguish themselves from their European counterparts, turned to the more remote regions of the country (meaning the West) to find appropriate subjects. The short story was a highly popular medium among those American writers who between 1865 and the 1890s formed the literary movement referred to as the local-color movement. Local-color stories were characterized by a focus on regional settings and representations of customs, costumes, and dialects of the people living there. Obviously, American Indians provided the local colorists with just the kind of home-based exoticism they were looking for.

Toward the end of the nineteenth century, the budding profession of anthropology brought about a more scientific approach to the study of the Indian. Following in the footsteps of Franz Boas, American anthropologists were soon busy all over the reservations, recording traditional life-styles that they believed were likely soon to disappear forever. These scholarly endeavors were eclipsed at the turn of the century by a veritable collecting craze that broke out nationwide. Indian artifacts became sought-after items for the interior decoration of middle-class homes or as mementos of the Wild West. Indian woodsmanship also became a topic of interest with the surge of a back-to-nature movement at that time, especially in conjunction with the founding of the Boy Scouts of America.[9] All of this generated a wider interest in Indians but one that was still limited by its almost exclusive concern for the past.

The situation also spurred the market for Indian writings; articles by or about Indians began to appear regularly in major American magazines like *Harper's*, *Sunset*, and the *Ladies Home Journal*. As

mentioned above, nonfiction continued to predominate, but a few
authors did at least respond to the popularization of the short-story
genre. Both the local-color movement and the new field of anthropology influenced their early productions, in which a concern for
ethnographic detail is often evident. Many of the stories were written specifically for juvenile magazines; in this context, which usually
included an appended moral text, they fulfilled a pedagogical function. Occasionally stories described contemporary reservation life,
a practice that became more common as disenchantment with allotment policies grew.

In view of the simple fact that the Indian writers of this period
wrote almost entirely for the non-Indian reader (Alex Posey is a
notable exception to this), it is not surprising to find popular stereo-
types sometimes reflected in their short stories. This is particularly
true of stories dealing with past lifestyles, in which the Indian protagonists often display characteristics of the European noble-savage
tradition. It should be remembered, however, that a nostalgic view
of the past was also a sincere expression of the Indian writers'
own feelings on the matter, not simply the adoption of an imposed
stereotype. On the other hand, those stories describing contemporary Indian life, and these make up the better half of this anthology,
can be said to represent a conscious effort on the part of the authors
to educate their readers concerning everyday Indian existence and
the problems resulting from cultural contact. As such, they are
atypical Indian stories for the times and may openly run counter to
current stereotypical expectations.

It is appropriate in more ways than one that this anthology should
begin with a story by Susette La Flesche. The story, "Nedawi,"
was originally published in 1881 in *St. Nicholas* magazine, one of
the more popular magazines for children. It is probably the first
nonlegend short story written by an Indian, and the gender of the
author also reflects the ever-increasing presence of women in both
Indian and American literature (women were particularly conspicuous during this period as fiction writers). Known widely as "Bright
Eyes," Susette La Flesche had become a public figure when she par-
ticipated in the Ponca case and was thus a forerunner of the writers

in the era that was about to unfold. In an article for the *Christian Union* in 1880, for example, she had already pointed out the need for better educational facilities for Indians and the advantages of citizenship—objectives that the SAI adopted some thirty years later.[10] Subtitled "An Indian Story from Real Life," "Nedawi" exemplifies much of Indian fiction published prior to the 1920s in its nostalgic description of a past way of life, emphasis on ethnographic detail, moralistic tone, and simplistic execution directed at the juvenile reader.

Indian women are further represented here by Pauline Johnson, Angel DeCora, and Gertrude Bonnin. "A Red Girl's Reasoning" was Pauline Johnson's first work of fiction, and it promptly received an award from the Canadian magazine *Dominion Illustrated* in 1893. It brings to Indian fiction the crucial theme of cultural marginality, which had first been touched on in William Apes's autobiography *A Son of the Forest* (1829).[11] Being of mixed ancestry herself, Johnson here presents a highly personalized version of the "half-breed," a popular fictional character in the nineteenth century.[12] Her own insecurity is indicated by her idealization of the mixed-blood protagonist in this story, to the point of nearly creating a stereotype in reverse. The predicament of a mixed-blood caught in a cultural limbo between two obviously incompatible cultures—a common experience for many Indian authors—would be a dominant theme in Indian fiction from the 1930s to the present.

A similar theme runs through Angel DeCora's sketch "The Sick Child," first published in *Harper's Monthly* in 1899. Although it describes the concrete issue of the high rate of child mortality on the reservation, the medicine man's loss of his healing power when confronted by what is presumably an imported disease conveys an equally serious disruption. The child narrator experiences not only the decimation of her family but also the impotence of traditional beliefs in a transformed world.

Gertrude Bonnin's reaction to transculturation was often more pronounced than that of her contemporaries. The mixed-blood protagonist in "The Soft-Hearted Sioux," published in *Harper's Monthly* in 1901, is unable to function in either culture, and Bonnin leaves him no other option than to make an honorable exit in a violent death. As in the Johnson story, the main character here seems somewhat unfinished or shallow, perhaps indicating a lack of sufficient artistic distance on the part of the author.

The apparent inevitability of tragedy in these stories stands in marked contrast to the successful "long way back" of the acculturated protagonists in modern Indian fiction, such as those in N. Scott Momaday's *House Made of Dawn* and Leslie M. Silko's *Ceremony*. Despite this seemingly fatalistic view, the stories by Johnson, DeCora, and Bonnin mentioned above are dynamic in the sense that they add a psychological depth to the Indian literature of the times that is often lacking in the more popular local-color pieces.

Both Gertrude Bonnin and Pauline Johnson wrote extensively on the subject of Indian women, and two fictional examples of this writing are included here. "A Warrior's Daughter," published in *Everybody's Magazine* in 1902, is Bonnin's inverted version of the warrior stories often produced by her male contemporaries. This romantic narrative of an Indian heroine's brave deed is typical of the kind of short stories being published at the time—apart from the reversed role of the sexes. "The Tenas Klootchman" (1911) is one of the many pieces Pauline Johnson wrote for *The Mother's Magazine*. It is set in the Canadian Northwest, where she had traveled extensively in her role as a stage entertainer, and narrated in the "as told to" form she was to use so successfully in her collection of Squamish stories titled *Legends of Vancouver* (1911). This sensitive depiction of an Indian woman's emotional bonds to her adopted child is representative of the kind of "charming" writing that the general reader was more prepared to accept (in contrast to the tone of "Red Girl's Reasoning" or "The Soft-Hearted Sioux").

The contributions by William Jones and Francis La Flesche, in turn, reflect the authors' dedication to the field of anthropology. Perhaps following the example set by Adolph Bandelier and his ethnographic novel *The Delight Makers* (1890), Jones and La Flesche occasionally made use of fiction as a means of passing on information gathered in the course of their research. The two stories "In the Name of His Ancestor" and "The Heart of the Brave," published in the *Harvard Monthly* in 1899 and 1900, are standard versions of

Plains Indian warrior tales. These stories of wartime exploits were originally told to, and even dramatized for, an audience of peers likely to be already familiar with the details. They could be passed down through the generations and thus could also function as a legitimate record of tribal history. "The Story of a Vision" (*Southern Workman*, 1901) describes a less formal storytelling session featuring the quasi-universal figure of the "grandfather" as a transmitter of cultural heritage. La Flesche further endows the story with a sense of humor, a rather pervasive element in modern Indian literature that seems to challenge the widespread stereotype of the stoic Indian. All three, of course, are adaptations of oral traditions to the written, short-story format, even though parts of them may well have originated in the authors' imagination.[13]

Alexander Posey stands out from among other Indian literates, then and now. His Fus Fixico letters are closer to the works of American satirists such as Seba Smith, James Russell Lowell, Finley Peter Dunne, and even Mark Twain. The letters' standard set of characters—Wolf Warrior, Kono Harjo, Tokpafka Micco, and Hotgun—are elderly Creek men who quip about all sorts of local issues. Many of the letters contain dialogue and read much like a short story. Although Posey wrote almost exclusively for local readers, his letters were quite popular among easterners as well, and some even found their way into newspapers in England. In the first letter included here, the four standard characters discuss the question of who really "pioneered" the Indian Territory; in the second one they ridicule the repeated and drawn-out conventions held between 1906 and 1907 in preparation for Oklahoma's statehood. The allotment of Indian lands, which resulted in the Snake Rebellion, led by Chitto Harjo in 1901, and the merging of the Indian Territory with Oklahoma Territory to form the state of Oklahoma in 1907 are common topics in his letters. They were published primarily in Indian Territory newspapers, like the Eufaula *Indian Journal*, which Posey edited for some time.

Along with Pauline Johnson, Charles A. Eastman and John M. Oskison were the most prolific and successful short-story writers of Indian descent during the first two decades of this century. Whereas the latter is now virtually unknown, Eastman's works continue to attract readers throughout the world. Most of his stories are for children and are either autobiographical sketches from his Sioux childhood, warrior tales, or accounts of hunter-animal encounters. His frequent idealization of the relationship between Indians and nature shows an affinity with the aforementioned back-to-nature movement that is corroborated by his own long involvement with the Boy Scouts. "The Gray Chieftain" is typical of his hunter-animal stories. The popularity of this type of story is indicated by the fact that it was published first in *Harper's Monthly* in 1904 and then included in William Dean Howells and Henry Mills Alden's anthology *Under the Sunset*, published in 1906. "The Singing Spirit" differs somewhat from his usual productions in having a more intricate plot. It combines elements from his warrior and hunter-animal repertoire but then branches off into a curious encounter between a Canadian métis (mixed-blood) protagonist and a party of Sioux who eventually adopt him. It appeared in *Sunset* (1907–8), a magazine that, along with *Harper's Monthly*, was quite open to Indian writing.

Oskison's output in short stories was equaled only by Pauline Johnson; both were truly professionals as far as this genre is concerned. Nearly all of Oskison's fiction is set in western frontier towns or eastern industrial cities and only a few stories have an Indian subject. Curiously enough, these happen to be among his better work and transcend the usual limitations of local-color stories. Some stories, in fact, reflect the progress that is evident in the development from the local-color stories to the regionalist writings of the 1920s and 1930s, as represented by authors like Mary Austin. This simply means that Oskison seems to place more emphasis on the psychological or sociological characteristics of a region rather than the mere details of its history and folkways. In a sense, his Indian stories resemble Johnson's "A Red Girl's Reasoning," but they avoid any hint of the emotional involvement of the latter. "The Problem of Old Harjo," which Oskison wrote for the *Southern Workman* in 1907, is one of his earlier pieces. In it, missionary aversion to the practice of polygamy ironically results in a reversed "conversion." "The Singing Bird" appears to have been Oskison's last short story. It was published in *Sunset* in 1925, after which he turned to writing novels. Here, the fidelity of a young Cherokee wife proves strong enough to resist the approaches of a mixed-blood, who personifies the challenges to traditional norms presented by Anglo society. Both pieces underline the vitality of Indian ways and thus reflect yet another transition in the history of Indian-white relations.

The notorious 1920s were a period of far-reaching change. The Western nations' self-aggrandizing views of their level of civilization had been challenged by the horrors of the first mass-production war and would soon be further stunted by the Great Depression. Intellectually, the American Dream was being questioned by young American authors who chose to live in Europe as expatriates. Even the notion of an American melting pot could not prevail in the face of mass immigration from eastern Europe. In the social sciences, Boasian cultural pluralism was establishing itself as an alternative to social Darwinism, which had so dominated the allotment era for America's Indians.

In the wake of so much uncertainty, the apparent stability of Indian ways made a favorable impression on some of America's intellectuals. A number of noted writers and artists, for instance, withdrew to the Southwest, where they came to be inspired by the various Pueblo cultures. When in 1921 the notorious Bursum Bill threatened to erode Pueblo landholdings, many of them joined forces to mobilize public support against it, and it was ultimately defeated. Two years later, so-called Red Progressives under the leadership of future commissioner of Indian affairs John Collier founded the American Indian Defense Association to pressure Congress to modify its Indian policy. Suddenly, the very traditions that had previously been condemned as impediments to Indian progress and prohibited by law received the sanction of a new reform outlook.

The Wheeler-Howard Act (or Indian Reorganization Act) of 1934 sought to reverse some of the allotment-era policies. It was also supported by several members of the Society of American Indians, including such prominent writers as Charles Eastman and Henry Roe Cloud (1884–1950). They had personally witnessed the disastrous results of the Dawes Act—despite citizenship, higher education, and professional training the Indian still remained a second-class being whose situation had become worse than ever before. Charles Eastman, for example, whom the reformers had held up as the example for the success of their policies, never really managed to establish himself professionally even though he held a medical degree. The ideals of the 1880s and 1890s proved to be much less viable than a pragmatic concern for Indian lands and resources. Indian writers inevitably came to have second thoughts about the supposed benefits of the system they had worked so hard to adapt to. They too began to reevaluate their cultural heritage.[14]

In fiction, the 1920s brought a shift in focus from the short story to the novel. This development had been foreshadowed first by John R. Ridge's 1854 romance, *The Life and Adventures of Joaquin Murieta*, and more recently by Simon Pokagon's fictional autobiography, *Queen of the Woods* (1899). These works were followed by John M. Oskison's *Wild Harvest* (1925), *Black Jack Davy* (1926), and *Brothers Three* (1935); Mourning Dove's *Cogewea, the Half-Blood* (1927); John Joseph Mathews's *Sundown* (1934); and D'Arcy McNickle's *The Surrounded* (1936).[15] Short stories by Indians appeared only sporadically and thus seem to have lost their appeal among major magazines. Interestingly enough, this occurred precisely at the time when the American short story was reaching the zenith of its literary development.

John Joseph Mathews and D'Arcy McNickle are the most prominent Indian writers of the New Deal era. Both actively supported Collier's administration in the Bureau of Indian Affairs (BIA) and personally helped to implement its policies. Both also began their literary careers writing fiction but found more recognition finally as historians. Since Mathews and McNickle published works as late as the 1970s, they can be viewed as a link between early and contemporary Indian literature. Their writings fully reflect the Indian self-consciousness of modern times and thus represent a marked departure from the trends of previous decades.

"Ee Sa Rah N'eah's Story" is one of several sketches Mathews wrote for the University of Oklahoma's *Sooner Magazine*, most of which depict hunting adventures and have no Indian connection. In its use of dialect and humor, this story is somewhat reminiscent of

Posey, even though it makes no political statement per se. Mathews published it in 1931, when he was in the process of rediscovering his Osage heritage and was about to launch his career as a historian of that tribe.

"Train Time" by McNickle originally appeared in a BIA publication titled *Indians at Work.* Lack of understanding and communication between members of different cultures is a prevalent topic in McNickle's fiction, including his great novel *Wind from an Enemy Sky* (1978, posthumous). The Anglo protagonists of his stories often bring about disaster despite their good intentions because they prove unable to comprehend or accept values that differ from their own. In "Hard Riding," one of McNickle's better short stories, written sometime in the 1920s or 1930s but never published, the Indian victims of such misguided Anglo goodwill are able to avert possible conflicts in tricksterlike fashion. It is a wonderfully humorous account of Indian resilience and is therefore an appropriate close for this anthology.

The stories gathered here constitute a prelude to the real blossoming of Indian fiction in the late 1960s. Although the novel has come to be the most popular genre, the short story has also experienced a boom during the last two decades, as evidenced by the publication of Kenneth Rosen's *The Man to Send Rain Clouds* (1974) and Simon Ortiz's more recent and inclusive *Earth Power Coming* (1983).[16]

Contemporary fiction is no longer a mere by-product of Indian literature; on the contrary, judging by the literary awards, the sales figures, and the number of translations, it has obviously become the dominant genre for the general reading public. Works by N. Scott Momaday, Leslie Silko, James Welch, Gerald Vizenor, and Louise Erdrich have even found acceptance as classics of modern American fiction. The thematic content of their novels and short stories is unique, yet it is universal enough to move beyond the limitations of local-color or "folk" literature. Whereas previous generations of Indian authors apparently were careful to keep oral tradition and the act of writing fiction separate, today's poets, novelists, and short-story writers do not hesitate to merge the two forms into a new and exciting literary product. It is as if past and present were finally reconciled by a process of artistic development, one in which the writers included here had a definite part.

NOTES

1. See David H. Brumble, *An Annotated Bibliography of American Indian and Eskimo Autobiographies* (Lincoln: University of Nebraska Press, 1981); and Daniel F. Littlefield and James W. Parins, comps., *A Bio-Bibliography of Native American Writers, 1772–1924* (Metuchen, N.J.: Scarecrow Press, 1981; supplement published in 1985). For an inclusive historical outline, see La Vonne Brown Ruoff, "Old Traditions and New Forms," in Paula Gunn Allen, ed., *Studies in American Indian Literature* (New York: Modern Language Association, 1983), 147–168; and idem, "American Indian Literature: Introduction and Bibliography," *American Studies International* 24 (October 1986): 2–52.

2. For references on oral literature, see William M. Clements and Francis M. Malpezzi, *Native American Folklore, 1879–1979: An Annotated Bibliography* (Athens: Ohio University/Swallow Press, 1984).

3. Samson Occom, *A Sermon, Preached at the Execution of Moses Paul, an Indian* (New Haven, Conn.: Press of Thomas and Samuel Green, 1772). Earlier writings are available in the form of letters; see Walter T. Meserve, "English Works of Seventeenth-Century Indians," *American Quarterly* 8 (Fall 1956): 264–277.

4. Roy Harvey Pearce, *Savagism and Civilization* (Baltimore: Johns Hopkins University Press, 1953). See also Robert Berkhofer, Jr., *The White Man's Indian: Images of the American Indian from Columbus to the Present* (New York: Knopf, 1978).

5. David Cusick, *Sketches of the Ancient History of the Six Nations* (Lewiston, N.Y.: By the Author, 1827); George Copway, *The Traditional History and Characteristic Sketches of the Ojibway Nation* (London: Gilpin, 1850).

6. Elias Boudinot, *Poor Sarah; or, Religion Exemplified in the Life and Death of an Indian Woman* (Mt. Pleasant, Ohio: Elisha Bates, 1823); John R. Ridge, *The Life and Adventures of Joaquin Murieta*, 3d ed. (San Francisco: F. MacCrellich and Co., 1874; 1st ed., 1854; reprint, Norman: University of Oklahoma Press, 1977); Theda Perdue, *Cherokee Editor: The Writings of Elias Boudinot* (Knoxville: University of Tennessee Press, 1983). John R. Ridge (1827–1867) also published *Poems* (San Francisco: Henry Payot and Co., 1868), as well as a number of essays collected by David Farmer and

Rennard Strickland in *A Trumpet of Our Own: Yellow Bird's Essays on the North American Indian* (San Francisco: Book Club of California, 1981).

7. Figures taken from Frederick E. Hoxie, *A Final Promise: The Campaign to Assimilate the Indians, 1880–1920* (Lincoln: University of Nebraska Press, 1984).

8. For a good survey of this period, see Hazel Hertzberg, *The Search for an American Indian Identity: Modern Pan-Indian Movements* (Syracuse: Syracuse University Press, 1971).

9. Roderick Nash, *Wilderness and the American Mind*, 2d ed. (New Haven, Conn.: Yale University Press, 1974).

10. "The Indian Question," *Christian Union*, March 10, 1880.

11. William Apes, *A Son of the Forest: The Experience of William Apes, a Native of the Forest, Comprising a Notice of the Pequot Tribe of Indians* (New York: By the Author, 1829; reprint, 1831).

12. William J. Scheick, *The Half-Blood: A Cultural Symbol in Nineteenth-Century American Fiction* (Lexington: University Press of Kentucky, 1979).

13. Charles Eastman's "The Madness of Bald Eagle" (*Southern Workman* 34 [March 1905]: 141–143) relates the Sioux version of an event nearly identical to the one described in Jones's "In the Name of His Ancestor."

14. It is interesting, for example, to note some of the differences in outlook between Eastman's first autobiographical volume, *Indian Boyhood* (1902), and *From the Deep Woods to Civilization*, which he wrote in 1916. His views of "civilization" in the latter, for instance, are no longer as unreflectively optimistic as they were in his "First Impressions."

15. Most of these novels are discussed in Charles R. Larson, *American Indian Fiction* (Albuquerque: University of New Mexico Press, 1978).

16. Kenneth Rosen, ed., *The Man to Send Rain Clouds: Contemporary Stories by American Indians* (New York: Vintage Books, 1974); Simon Ortiz, ed., *Earth Power Coming: Short Fiction in Native American Literature* (Tsaile, Ariz.: Navajo Community College, 1983).

The Singing Spirit

Susette La Flesche

Susette La Flesche was born in 1854 on the Omaha Reservation in what is now Nebraska. She was the oldest of Joseph La Flesche's daughters by his first wife, Mary Gale, and was a stepsister of Francis La Flesche. Her Omaha name was Inshata Theumba (Bright Eyes).

Until 1869 she attended the Presbyterian Mission School irregularly, and from 1872 to 1875 she was a student at the Elizabeth Institute for Young Ladies, in New Jersey. Following her return to the reservation, she took up teaching and conducted a Sunday school for Omaha children from 1877 to 1879.

Susette La Flesche became involved in the controversy over the Ponca removal and, together with Francis La Flesche, accompanied Luther Standing Bear on his tour to generate public support in 1879 and 1880. At this time she began to speak publicly on Indian affairs and soon became very popular among eastern audiences. During the tour she met philanthropist and journalist Thomas H. Tibbles, whom she married in 1881.

From 1883 to 1885 she lived with her husband in Washington, D.C., where she continued to lecture on Indian subjects and wrote occasional articles and stories. In 1885 they both returned to the Omaha Reservation to farm her allotment. Two years later her husband accepted a post as a reporter for the *Omaha Herald*. In December 1890 she and her husband visited the Pine Ridge Agency, where they witnessed the tragedy of Wounded Knee.

After another brief sojourn in Washington, the couple moved to Lincoln, Nebraska, in 1894 to take over the editorship of the *Weekly Independent*, a Populist newspaper. La Flesche herself edited the newspaper initially. Due to her ailing health, she and her husband returned to their farm in Logan Valley around 1895.

Aside from a number of articles and stories, most of which have gone unrecorded, she also cooperated with Fannie Reed Griffin to produce *Oo-mah-ha Ta-wa-tha*, which was published for the Trans-Mississippi Exposition in 1898. She wrote at least one of the chapters in the booklet and did the illustrations, including two color prints. In addition, she wrote the introduction to Thomas Tibbles's *The Ponca Chiefs* (1880) and *Ploughed Under* (1881). La Flesche died on May 26, 1903, at her home in Nebraska.

REFERENCES

Clark, Jerry E., and Martha Ellen Webb. "Susette and Susan La Flesche: Reformer and Missionary." In James A. Clifton, ed., *Being and Becoming Indian: Biographical Studies of North American Frontiers*, 137–159. Chicago: Dorsey Press, 1989.
Crary, Margaret. *Susette La Flesche: Voice of the Omaha Indians*. New York: Hawthorn, 1973. A biographical novel.
Green, Norma K. "Four Sisters: Daughters of Joseph La Flesche." *Nebraska History* 45 (June 1964): 165–176.
———. *Iron Eye's Family: The Children of Joseph La Flesche*. Lincoln, Nebr.: Johnson Publishing Company, 1969.

STORIES BY SUSETTE LA FLESCHE

"Nedawi." *St. Nicholas* 8 (January 1881): 225–230.
"Omaha Legends and Tent Stories." *Wide Awake* 17 (June 1883): 21–25.

Nedawi

"BRIGHT EYES" [SUSETTE LA FLESCHE]

"Nedawi!" called her mother, "take your little brother while I go with your sister for some wood." Nedawi ran into the tent, bringing back her little red blanket, but the brown-faced, roly-poly baby, who had been having a comfortable nap in spite of being all the while tied straight to his board, woke with a merry crow just as the mother was about to attach him, board and all, to Nedawi's neck. So he was taken from the board instead, and, after he had kicked in happy freedom for a moment, Nedawi stood in front of her mother, who placed Habazhu on the little girl's back, and drew the blanket over him, leaving his arms free. She next put into his hand a little hollow gourd, filled with seeds, which served as a rattle; Nedawi held both ends of the blanket tightly in front of her, and was then ready to walk around with the little man.

Where should she go? Yonder was a group of young girls playing a game of *konci*, or dice. The dice were five plum-seeds, scorched black, and had little stars and quarter-moons instead of numbers. She went over and stood by the group, gently rocking herself from side to side, pretty much as white children do when reciting the multiplication table. The girls would toss up the wooden bowl, letting it drop with a gentle thud on the pillow beneath, the falling dice making a pleasant clatter which the baby liked to hear. The stakes were a little heap of beads, rings, and bracelets. The laughter and exclamations of the girls, as some successful toss brought down the dice three stars and two quarter-moons (the highest throw), made Nedawi wish that she, too, were a young girl, and could win and wear all those pretty things. How gay she would look! Just then, the little glittering heap caught baby's eye. He tried to wriggle out of the blanket to get to it, but Nedawi held tight. Then he set up a yell. Nedawi walked away very reluctantly, because she wanted to stay

3

and see who would win. She went to her mother's tent, but found it deserted. Her father and brothers had gone to the chase. A herd of buffalo had been seen that morning, and all the men in the tribe had gone, and would not be back till night. Her mother, her sister, and the women of the household had gone to the river for wood and water. The tent looked enticingly cool, with the sides turned up to let the breeze sweep through, and the straw mats and soft robes seemed to invite her to lie down on them and dream the afternoon away, as she was too apt to do. She did not yield to the temptation, however, for she knew Mother would not like it, but walked over to her cousin Metai's tent. She found her cousin "keeping house" with a number of little girls, and stood to watch them while they put up little tents, just large enough to hold one or two girls.

"Nedawi, come and play," said Metai. "You can make the fire and cook. I'll ask Mother for something to cook."

"But what shall I do with Habazhu?" said Nedawi.

"I'll tell you. Put him in my tent, and make believe he's our little old grandfather."

Forthwith he was transferred from Nedawi's back to the little tent. But Habazhu had a decided objection to staying in the dark little place, where he could not see anything, and crept out of the door on his hands and knees. Nedawi collected a little heap of sticks, all ready for the fire, and went off to get a fire-brand to light it with. While she was gone, Habazhu crawled up to a bowl of water which stood by the intended fire-place, and began dabbling in it with his chubby little hands, splashing the water all over the sticks prepared for the fire. Then he thought he would like a drink. He tried to lift the bowl in both hands, but only succeeded in spilling the water over himself and the fire-place.

When Nedawi returned, she stood aghast; then, throwing down the brand, she took her little brother by the shoulders and, I am sorry to say, shook him violently, jerked him up, and dumped him down by the door of the little tent from which he had crawled. "You bad little boy!" she said. "It's too bad that I have to take care of you when I want to play."

You see, she was no more perfect than any little white girl who gets into a temper now and then. The baby's lip quivered, and he began to cry. Metai said to Nedawi: "I think it's real mean for you to shake him, when he doesn't know any better."

Metai picked up Baby and tried to comfort him. She kissed him over and over, and talked to him in baby language. Nedawi's conscience, if the little savage could be said to have any, was troubling her. She loved her baby brother dearly, even though she did get out of patience with him now and then.

"I'll put a clean little shirt on him and pack him again," said she, suddenly. Then she took off his little wet shirt, wrung it out, and spread it on the tall grass to dry in the sun. Then she went home, and, going to a pretty painted skin in which her mother kept his clothes, she selected the red shirt, which she thought was the prettiest. She was in such a hurry, however, that she forgot to close and tie up the skin again, and she carelessly left his clean shirts lying around as she had laid them out. When Baby was on her back again, she walked around with him, giving directions and overseeing the other girls at their play, determined to do that rather than nothing.

The other children were good-natured, and took her ordering as gracefully as they could. Metai made the fire in a new place, and then went to ask her mother to give her something to cook. Her mother gave her a piece of dried buffalo meat, as hard as a chip and as brittle as glass. Metai broke it up into small pieces, and put the pieces into a little tin pail of water, which she hung over the fire. "Now," she said, "when the meat is cooked and the soup is made, I will call you all to a feast, and Habazhu shall be the chief."

They all laughed. But alas for human calculations! During the last few minutes, a shy little girl, with soft, wistful black eyes, had been watching them from a little distance. She had on a faded, shabby blanket and a ragged dress.

"Metai," said Nedawi, "let's ask that girl to play with us; she looks so lonesome."

"Well," said Metai, doubtfully, "I don't care; but my mother said she didn't want me to play with ragged little girls."

"My father says we must be kind to poor little girls, and help them all we can; so *I'm* going to play with her if *you* don't," said Nedawi, loftily.

Although Metai was the hostess, Nedawi was the leading spirit, and had her own way, as usual. She walked up to the little creature and said, "Come and play with us, if you want to." The little girl's eyes brightened, and she laughed. Then she suddenly drew from under her blanket a pretty bark basket, filled with the most delicious red and yellow plums. "My brother picked them in the woods, and I give them to you," was all she said. Nedawi managed to free one hand, and took the offering with an exclamation of delight, which drew the other girls quickly around. Instead of saying "Oh! Oh!" as you would have said, they cried "Hin! Hin!" which expressed their feeling quite as well, perhaps.

"Let us have them for our feast," said Metai, taking them.

Little Indian children are taught to share everything with one another, so it did not seem strange to Nedawi to have her gift looked on as common property. But, while the attention of the little group had been concentrated on the matter in hand, a party of mischievous boys, passing by, caught sight of the little tents and the tin pail hanging over the fire. Simultaneously, they set up a war-whoop and, dashing into the deserted camp, they sent the tent-poles scattering right and left, and snatching up whatever they could lay hands on, including the tin pail and its contents, they retreated. The little girls, startled by the sudden raid on their property, looked up. Rage possessed their little souls. Giving shrieks of anger, they started in pursuit. What did Nedawi do? She forgot plums, baby, and everything. The ends of the blanket slipped from her grasp, and she darted forward like an arrow after her companions.

Finding the chase hopeless, the little girls came to a stand-still, and some of them began to cry. The boys had stopped, too; and seeing the tears flow, being good-hearted boys in spite of their mischief, they surrendered at discretion. They threw back the articles they had taken, not daring to come near. They did not consider it manly for big boys like themselves to strike or hurt little girls, even though they delighted in teasing them, and they knew from experience that they would be at the mercy of the offended party if they went near enough to be touched. The boy who had the dinner brought the little pail which had contained it as near as he dared, and setting it down ran away.

"You have spilt all our soup. There's hardly any of it left. You bad boys!" said one of the girls.

They crowded around with lamentations over their lost dinner. The boys began to feel remorseful.

"Let's go into the woods and get them some plums to make up for it."

"Say, girls, hand us your pail, and we'll fill it up with plums for you."

So the affair was settled.

But, meanwhile, what became of the baby left so unceremoniously in the tall grass? First he opened his black eyes wide at this style of treatment. He was not used to it. Before he had time, however, to make up his mind whether to laugh or cry, his mother came to the rescue. She had just come home and thrown the wood off her back, when she caught sight of Nedawi dropping him. She ran to pick him up, and finding him unhurt, kissed him over and over. Some of the neighbors had run up to see what was the matter. She said to them:

"I never did see such a thoughtless, heedless child as my Nedawi. She really has 'no ears.' I don't know what in the world will ever become of her. When something new interests her, she forgets everything else. It was just like her to act in this way."

Then they all laughed, and one of them said:

"Never mind—she will grow wiser as she grows older," after which consoling remark they went away to their own tents.

It was of no use to call Nedawi back. She was too far off.

Habazhu was given over to the care of the nurse, who had just returned from her visit. An hour or two after, Nedawi came home.

"Mother!" she exclaimed, as she saw her mother frying bread for supper, "I am so hungry. Can I have some of that bread?"

"Where is your little brother?" was the unexpected reply.

Nedawi started. Where *had* she left him? She tried to think.

"Why, Mother, the last I remember I was packing him, and—and oh, Mother! you *know* where he is. Please tell me."

"When you find him and bring him back to me, perhaps I shall forgive you," was the cold reply.

This was dreadful. Her mother had never treated her in that way before. She burst into tears, and started out to find Habazhu, crying all the way. She knew that her mother knew where baby was, or she would not have taken it so coolly; and she knew also that her mother expected her to bring him home. As she went stumbling along through the grass, she felt herself seized and held in somebody's strong arms, and a great, round, hearty voice said:

"What's the matter with my little niece? Have all her friends deserted her that she is wailing like this? Or has her little dog died? I thought Nedawi was a brave little woman."

It was her uncle Two Crows. She managed to tell him, through her sobs, the whole story. She knew, if she told him herself, he would not laugh at her about it, for he would sympathize in her troubles, though he was a great tease. When she ceased, he said to her: "Well, your mother wants you to be more careful next time, I suppose; and, by the way, I think I saw a little boy who looked very much like Habazhu, in my tent."

Sure enough, she found him there with his nurse. When she got home with them, she found her mother,—her own dear self,—and, after giving her a big hug, she sat quietly down by the fire, resolved to be very good in the future. She did not sit long, however, for soon a neighing of horses, and the running of girls and children through the camp to meet the hunters, proclaimed their return. All was bustle and gladness throughout the camp. There had been a successful chase, and the led horses were laden with buffalo meat. These horses were led by the young girls to the tents to be unpacked, while the boys took the hunting-horses to water and tether in the grass. Fathers, as they dismounted, took their little children in their arms, tired as they were. Nedawi was as happy as any in the camp, for her seventeen-year-old brother, White Hawk, had killed his first buffalo, and had declared that the skin should become Nedawi's robe, as soon as it was tanned and painted.

What a pleasant evening that was to Nedawi, when the whole family sat around a great fire, roasting the huge buffalo ribs, and she played with her little brother Habazhu, stopping now and then to listen to the adventures of the day, which her father and brothers were relating! The scene was truly a delightful one, the camp-fires lighting up the pleasant family groups here and there, as the flames rose and fell. The bit of prairie where the tribe had camped had a clear little stream running through it, with shadowy hills around, while over all hung the clear, star-lit sky. It seemed as if nature were trying to protect the poor waifs of humanity clustered in that spot. Nedawi felt the beauty of the scene, and was just thinking of nestling down by her father to enjoy it dreamily, when her brothers called for a dance. The little drum was brought forth, and Nedawi danced to its accompaniment and her brothers' singing. She danced gravely, as became a little maiden whose duty it was to entertain the family circle. While she was dancing, a little boy, about her own age, was seen hovering near. He would appear, and, when spoken to, would disappear in the tall, thick grass.

It was Mischief, a playmate of Nedawi's. Everybody called him "Mischief," because mischief appeared in every action of his. It shone from his eyes and played all over his face.

"You little plague," said White Hawk; "what do you want?"

For answer, the "little plague" turned a somersault just out of White Hawk's reach. When the singing was resumed, Mischief crept quietly up behind White Hawk, and, keeping just within the shadow, mimicked Nedawi's grave dancing, and he looked so funny that Nedawi suddenly laughed, which was precisely Mischief's object. But before he could get out of reach, as he intended, Thunder, Nedawi's other brother, who had been having an eye on him, clutched tight hold of him, and Mischief was landed in front of the fire-place, in full view of the whole family. "Now," said Thunder, "you are my prisoner. You stay there and dance with Nedawi." Mischief knew there was no escape, so he submitted with a good grace. He went through all sorts of antics, shaking his fists in the air, twirling suddenly around and putting his head close to the ground, keeping time with the accompaniment through it all.

Nedawi danced staidly on, now and then frowning at him; but she knew of old that he was irrepressible. When Nedawi sat down, he threw into her lap a little dark something and was off like a shot, yelling at the top of his voice, either in triumph at his recent achievements or as a practice for future war-whoops.

"Nedawi, what is it?" said her mother.

Nedawi took it to the fire, when the something proved to be a poor little bird.

"I thought he had something in his hand when he was shaking his fist in the air," said Nedawi's sister, Nazainza, laughing.

"Poor little thing!" said Nedawi; "it is almost dead."

She put its bill into the water, and tenderly tried to make it drink. The water seemed to revive it somewhat.

"I'll wrap it up in something warm," said Nedawi, "and maybe it will sing in the morning."

"Let me see it," said Nedawi's father.

Nedawi carried it to him.

"Don't you feel sorry for it, daughter?"

"Yes, Father," she answered.

"Then take it to the tall grass, yonder, and put it down where no one will step on it, and, as you put it down, say: 'God, I give you back your little bird. As I pity it, pity me.'"

"And will God take care of it?" said Nedawi, reverently, and opening her black eyes wide at the thought.

"Yes," said her father.

"Well, I will do as you say," said Nedawi, and she walked slowly out of the tent.

Then she took it over to the tall, thick grass, and making a nice, cozy little nest for it, left it there, saying just what her father had told her to say. When she came back, she said:

"Father, I said it."

"That was right, little daughter," and Nedawi was happy at her father's commendation.

Nedawi always slept with her grandmother and sister, exactly in the middle of the circle formed by the wigwam, with her feet to the fire-place. That place in the tent was always her grandmother's place, just as the right-hand side of the tent was her father's and mother's, and the left-hand her brothers'. There never was any confusion. The tribe was divided into bands, and every band was composed of several families. Each band had its chief, and the whole tribe was ruled by the head-chief, who was Nedawi's father. He had his own particular band besides. Every tent had its own place in the band, and every band had its own particular place in the great circle forming the camp. Each chief was a representative, in council, of the men composing his band, while over all was the head-chief. The executive power was vested in the "soldiers' lodge," and when decisions were arrived at in council, it was the duty of its soldiers to execute all its orders, and punish all violations of the tribal laws. The office of "town-crier" was held by several old men, whose duty it was "to cry out" through the camp the announcements of councils, invitations to feasts, and to give notice of anything in which the whole tribe were called on to take part.

Well, before Nedawi went to sleep this evening, she hugged her grandmother, and said to her:

"Please tell me a story."

Her grandmother said:

"I cannot, because it is summer. In the winter I will tell you stories."

"Why not in summer?" said Nedawi.

"Because, when people tell stories and legends in summer, the snakes come around to listen. You don't want any snakes to come near us to-night, do you?"

"But," said Nedawi, "I have not seen any snakes for the longest time, and if you tell it right softly they won't hear you."

"Nedawi," said her mother, "don't bother your grandmother. She is tired and wants to sleep."

Thereupon Grandmother's heart felt sorry for her pet, and she said to Nedawi:

"Well, if you will keep still and go right to sleep when I am through, I will tell you how the turkeys came to have red eyelids.

"Once upon a time, there was an old woman living all alone with her grandson, Rabbit. He was noted for his cunning and for his tricks, which he played on everyone. One day, the old woman said to him, 'Grandson, I am hungry for some meat.' Then the boy took his bow and arrows, and in the evening he came home with a deer on his shoulders, which he threw at her feet, and said, 'Will that satisfy you?' She said, 'Yes, grandson.' They lived on that meat several days, and, when it was gone, she said to him again, 'Grandson,

I am hungry for some meat.' This time he went without his bow and arrows, but he took a bag with him. When he got into the woods, he called all the turkeys together. They gathered around him, and he said to them: 'I am going to sing to you, while you shut your eyes and dance. If one of you opens his eyes while I am singing, his eyelids shall turn red.' Then they all stood in a row, shut their eyes, as he had told them, and began to dance, and this is the song he sang to them while they danced:

> Ha! wadamba thike
> Inshta zhida, inshta zhida,
> Imba theonda,
> Imba theonda.

[The literal translation is:

> Ho! he who peeps
> Red eyes, red eyes,
> Flap your wings,
> Flap your wings.]

"Now, while they were dancing away, with their eyes shut, the boy took them, one by one, and put them into his bag. But the last one in the row began to think it very strange that his companions made no noise, so he gave one peep, screamed in his fright, 'They are making 'way with us!' and flew away. The boy took his bag of turkeys home to his grandmother, but ever after that the turkeys had red eyelids."

Nedawi gave a sigh of satisfaction when the story was finished, and would have asked for more, but just then her brothers came in from a dance which they had been attending in some neighbor's tent. She knew her lullaby time had come. Her brothers always sang before they slept either love or dancing songs, beating time on their breasts, the regular beats making a sort of accompaniment for the singing. Nedawi loved best of all to hear her father's war-songs, for he had a musical voice, and few were the evenings when she had gone to sleep without hearing a lullaby from her father or brothers. Among the Indians, it is the fathers who sing, instead of the mothers. Women sing only on state occasions, when the tribe have a great dance, or at something of the sort. Mothers "croon" their babies to sleep, instead of singing.

Gradually the singing ceased, and the brothers slept as well as Nedawi, and quiet reigned over the whole camp.

Pauline Johnson

Emily Pauline Johnson was born on March 10, 1861, on the Six Nations Reserve near Brantford, Ontario. Her father was the noted Mohawk leader and government interpreter George Henry Martin; her mother, Emily Susanna Howells, was of English descent and first cousin of William Dean Howells. Later in life Pauline Johnson took up her paternal grandfather's Indian name, Tekahionwake (Double Wampum).

Johnson received much of her education under the tutelage of her mother, who introduced her to the classics of English literature. She also received some instruction from a private governess prior to enrolling for three years at a Mohawk day school and for another two at the Brantford Collegiate.

Although she is primarily remembered today as a poet, in her own day she was known as a stage performer. She began her stage career in 1892, reciting some of her poems and later complementing her program with dramatic skits. For some fifteen years she toured throughout Canada, including some of its remotest northwestern regions, as well as the United States and England. She was considered to be one of Canada's most popular entertainers. During the 1893–94 season alone, she gave a total of 125 recitals. Finally, in 1909, she settled in Vancouver and turned to writing exclusively.

Johnson apparently published her first poem, "My Little Jean," in the New York–based *Gems of Poetry* in 1884. By 1889 she had established enough of a reputation to be included in William D. Lighthall's anthology of Canadian poets, *Songs of the Great Dominion* (London: W. Scott). In 1895, she published a much acclaimed collection of poems, *The White Wampum*, with one of England's most prestigious publishing firms, John Lane in London. Her second book of poems, *Canadian Born* (Toronto: George N. Morang &

Co., 1903), was not as successful as her first. Her poems were later published collectively in *Flint and Feather* (Toronto: Mousson Book Co., 1912; reprint, Markham, Ont.: PaperJacks, 1973).

In order to augment her meager earnings from poetry, Johnson turned increasingly to writing prose. In 1892 she began to write articles for Canada's *Dominion Illustrated* on Indian and regional Canadian subjects. In 1906 she also started to write short stories for the *Boy's World* and, in 1908 and 1909, for *Mother's Magazine*. Many of the former were collected in *The Shagganappi* (Toronto: William Briggs, 1913) and the latter in *The Moccasin Maker* (Toronto: William Briggs, 1913; reprint, Tucson: University of Arizona Press, 1987). Johnson also transcribed traditional Kutenai stories told to her by Joe Capilano. These were first published in 1910 and 1911 by the *Vancouver Province* and then collected in *Legends of Vancouver* (Vancouver: Sunset Publishing Co., 1911; reprint, Toronto: McClelland, 1961).

Johnson died on March 7, 1913, in Vancouver. For the centennial celebration of her birthday in 1961, her former home in Brantford was made into a national shrine, and a commemorative stamp was issued by the Canadian government in cooperation with the Institute of Iroquoian Studies.

REFERENCES

Foster, W. Garland. *The Mohawk Princess: Being Some Account of the Life of Tekahion-Wake (E. Pauline Johnson)*. Vancouver: Lion's Gate Publishing Co., 1931.

Keller, Betty. *Pauline: A Biography of Pauline Johnson*. Vancouver: Douglas & McIntyre, 1981.

McRaye, Walter. *Pauline Johnson and Her Friends*. Toronto: Ryerson Press, 1947. Personal, somewhat inaccurate account.

Ruoff, LaVonne Brown. Introduction to *The Moccasin Maker*, by E. Pauline Johnson. Tucson: University of Arizona Press, 1987.

Van Steen, Marcus. *Pauline Johnson: Her Life and Work*. Toronto: Mousson Book Company, 1965.

STORIES BY PAULINE JOHNSON

"A Red Girl's Reasoning." *Dominion Illustrated*, February 1893, 19–28.
"Maurice of His Majesty's Mails." *Boy's World*, June 23, 1906.
"The Saucy Seven." *Boy's World*, August 11, 1906.
"Dick Dines with His Dad." *Boy's World*, November 24, 1906.
"The Hero's Sacrifice." *Boy's World*, January 19, 1907.
"Grin Shy Billy." *Boy's World*, March 23, 1907.
"The Haunting Thaw." *Canadian Magazine*, May 1907, 20–22.
"The Broken String." *Boy's World*, July 27, 1907.
"The Home Comers." *Mother's Magazine*, September 1907, 4–6.
"Little Wolf-Willow." *Boy's World*, December 7, 1907.
"The Shadow Trail." *Boy's World*, December 21, 1907.
"A Night with North Eagle." *Boy's World*, January 18, 1908.
"Mother o' the Men: A Story of the Canadian North West Mounted
    Police." *Mother's Magazine*, February 1908, 14–16, 56.
"The Lieutenant Governor's Prize." *Boy's World*, June 20, 1908.
"The Scarlet Eye." *Boy's World*, August 1, 1908.
"The Cruise of the Brown One." *Boy's World*, September 12, 1908.
"The Envoy Extraordinary." *Mother's Magazine*, March 1909, 11–13.
"The Broken Barrels." *Boy's World*, March 27, 1909.
"The Whistling Swans." *Boy's World*, April 3, 1909.
"My Mother." *Mother's Magazine*, April 1909, 9–11; May 1909, 7–9, 14;
    June 1909, 10–12; July 1909, 15–18.
"The Delaware Idol." *Boy's World*, May 1, 1909.
"The King's Coin." *Boy's World*, May 29, 1909.
"Jack O'Lantern." *Boy's World*, October 30, 1909.
"The Christmas Heart." *Mother's Magazine*, December 1909, 13, 30.
"The Brotherhood." *Boy's World*, January 1, 1910.
"The Wolf Brothers." *Boy's World*, February 5, 1910.
"The Nest-Builder." *Mother's Magazine*, March 1910, 11, 32.
"The Call of the Skookum Chuck." *Mother's Magazine*, April 1910, 14–17.
"The Signal Code." *Boy's World*, July 16, 1910.
"The Barnardo Boy." *Boy's World*, August 13, 1910.
"The Potlach." *Boy's World*, October 8, 1910.
"Catherine of the Crow's Nest." *Mother's Magazine*, December 1910, 12–
    13, 29–30.
"Hoolool of the Totem Poles." *Mother's Magazine*, February 1911, 12–13,
    71.
"The Tenas Klootchman." *Mother's Magazine*, August 1911, 12–14.

A Red Girl's Reasoning

PAULINE JOHNSON

"Be pretty good to her, Charlie, my boy, or she'll balk sure as shooting."

That was what old Jimmy Robinson said to his brand new son-in-law, while they waited for the bride to reappear.

"Oh! you bet, there's no danger of much else. I'll be good to her, help me Heaven," replied Charlie McDonald, brightly.

"Yes, of course you will," answered the old man, "but don't you forget, there's a good big bit of her mother in her, and," closing his left eye significantly, "you don't understand these Indians as I do."

"But I'm just as fond of them, Mr. Robinson," Charlie said assertively, "and I get on with them too, now, don't I?"

"Yes, pretty well for a town boy; but when you have lived forty years among these people, as I have done; when you have had your wife as long as I have had mine—for there's no getting over it, Christine's disposition is as native as her mother's, every bit—and perhaps when you've owned for eighteen years a daughter as dutiful, as loving, as fearless, and, alas! as obstinate as that little piece you are stealing away from me today—I tell you, youngster, you'll know more than you know now. It is kindness for kindness, bullet for bullet, blood for blood. Remember, what you are, she will be," and the old Hudson Bay trader scrutinized Charlie McDonald's face like a detective.

It was a happy, fair face, good to look at, with a certain ripple of dimples somewhere about the mouth, and eyes that laughed out the very sunniness of their owner's soul. There was not a severe nor yet a weak line anywhere. He was a well-meaning young fellow, happily dispositioned, and a great favorite with the tribe at Robinson's Post, whither he had gone in the service of the Department of

Agriculture, to assist the local agent through the tedium of a long census-taking.

As a boy he had had the Indian relic-hunting craze, as a youth he had studied Indian archaeology and folk-lore, as a man he consummated his predilections for Indianology by loving, winning and marrying the quiet little daughter of the English trader, who himself had married a native woman twenty years ago. The country was all backwoods, and the Post miles and miles from even the semblance of civilization, and the lonely young Englishman's heart had gone out to the girl who, apart from speaking a very few words of English, was utterly uncivilized and uncultured, but had withal that marvellously innate refinement so universally possessed by the higher tribes of North American Indians.

Like all her race, observant, intuitive, having a horror of ridicule, consequently quick at acquirement and teachable in mental and social habits, she had developed from absolute pagan indifference into a sweet, elderly Christian woman, whose broken English, quiet manner, and still handsome copper-colored face, were the joy of old Robinson's declining years.

He had given their daughter Christine all the advantages of his own learning—which, if truthfully told, was not universal; but the girl had a fair common education, and the native adaptability to progress.

She belonged to neither and still to both types of the cultured Indian. The solemn, silent, almost heavy manner of the one so commingled with the gesticulating Frenchiness and vivacity of the other, that one unfamiliar with native Canadian life would find it difficult to determine her nationality.

She looked very pretty to Charles McDonald's loving eyes, as she reappeared in the doorway, holding her mother's hand and saying some happy words of farewell. Personally she looked much the same as her sisters, all Canada through, who are the offspring of red and white parentage—olive-complexioned, gray-eyed, black-haired, with figure slight and delicate, and the wistful, unfathomable expression in her whole face that turns one so heart-sick as they glance at the young Indians of today—it is the forerunner too frequently of "the white man's disease," consumption—but McDonald was pathetically in love, and thought her the most beautiful woman he had ever seen in his life.

There had not been much of a wedding ceremony. The priest had cantered through the service in Latin, pronounced the benediction in English, and congratulated the "happy couple" in Indian, as a compliment to the assembled tribe in the little amateur structure that did service at the post as a sanctuary.

But the knot was tied as firmly and indissolubly as if all Charlie McDonald's swell city friends had crushed themselves up against the chancel to congratulate him, and in his heart he was deeply thankful to escape the flower-pelting, white gloves, rice-throwing, and ponderous stupidity of a breakfast, and indeed all the regulation gimcracks of the usual marriage celebrations, and it was with a hand trembling with absolute happiness that he assisted his little Indian wife into the old muddy buckboard that, hitched to an underbred-looking pony, was to convey them over the first stages of their journey. Then came more adieus, some hand-clasping, old Jimmy Robinson looking very serious just at the last, Mrs. Jimmy, stout, stolid, betraying nothing of visible emotion, and then the pony, rough-shod and shaggy, trudged on, while mutual hand-waves were kept up until the old Hudson Bay Post dropped out of sight, and the buckboard with its lightsome load of hearts, deliriously happy, jogged on over the uneven trail.

She was "all the rage" that winter at the provincial capital. The men called her a "deuced fine little woman." The ladies said she was "just the sweetest wildflower." Whereas she was really but an ordinary, pale, dark girl who spoke slowly and with a strong accent, who danced fairly well, sang acceptably, and never stirred outside the door without her husband.

Charlie was proud of her; he was proud that she had "taken" so well among his friends, proud that she bore herself so complacently in the drawing-rooms of the wives of pompous Government officials, but doubly proud of her almost abject devotion to him. If ever human being was worshipped, that being was Charlie McDonald; it could scarcely have been otherwise, for the almost godlike strength of his passion for that little wife of his would have mastered and melted a far more invincible citadel than an already affectionate woman's heart.

Favorites socially, McDonald and his wife went everywhere. In fashionable circles she was "new"—a potent charm to acquire popularity, and the little velvet-clad figure was always the centre of interest among all the women in the room. She always dressed in velvet. No woman in Canada, has she but the faintest dash of native blood in her veins, but loves velvets and silks. As beef to the Englishman, wine to the Frenchman, fads to the Yankee, so are velvet and silk to the Indian girl, be she wild as prairie grass, be she on the borders of civilization, or, having stepped within its boundary, mounted the steps of culture even under its superficial heights.

"Such a dolling little appil blossom," said the wife of a local M.P., who brushed up her etiquette and English once a year at Ottawa. "Does she always laugh so sweetly, and gobble you up with those great big gray eyes of hers, when you are togetheah at home, Mr. McDonald? If so, I should think youah pooah brothah would feel himself terribly *de trop*."

He laughed lightly. "Yes, Mrs. Stuart, there are not two of Christie; she is the same at home and abroad, and as for Joe, he doesn't mind us a bit; he's no end fond of her."

"I'm very glad he is. I always fancied he did not care for her, d'you know."

If ever a blunt woman existed it was Mrs. Stuart. She really meant nothing, but her remark bothered Charlie. He was fond of his brother, and jealous for Christie's popularity. So that night when he and Joe were having a pipe he said:

"I've never asked you yet what you thought of her, Joe." A brief pause, then Joe spoke. "I'm glad she loves you."

"Why?"

"Because that girl has but two possibilities regarding humanity —love or hate."

"Humph! Does she love or hate *you*?"

"Ask her."

"You talk bosh. If she hated you, you'd get out. If she loved you I'd *make* you get out."

Joe McDonald whistled a little, then laughed.

"Now that we are on the subject; I might as well ask—honestly, old man, wouldn't you and Christie prefer keeping house alone to having me always around?"

"Nonsense, sheer nonsense. Why, thunder, man, Christie's no end fond of you, and as for me—you surely don't want assurances from me?"

"No, but I often think a young couple—"

"Young couple be blowed! After a while when they want you and your old surveying chains, and spindle-legged tripod telescope kickshaws, farther west, I venture to say the little woman will cry her eyes out—won't you, Christie?" This last in a higher tone, as through clouds of tobacco smoke he caught sight of his wife passing the doorway.

She entered. "Oh, no, I would not cry; I never do cry, but I would be heart-sore to lose you, Joe, and apart from that"—a little wickedly—"you may come in handy for an exchange some day, as Charlie does always say when he hoards up duplicate relics."

"Are Charlie and I duplicates?"

"Well—not exactly"—her head a little to one side, and eyeing them both merrily, while she slipped softly on to the arm of her husband's chair—"but, in the event of Charlie's failing me"—everyone laughed then. The "some day" that she spoke of was nearer than they thought. It came about in this wise.

There was a dance at the Lieutenant-Governor's, and the world and his wife were there. The nobs were in great feather that night, particularly the women, who flaunted about in new gowns and much splendor. Christie McDonald had a new gown also, but wore it with the utmost unconcern, and if she heard any of the flattering remarks made about her she at least appeared to disregard them.

"I never dreamed you could wear blue so splendidly," said Captain Logan, as they sat out a dance together.

"Indeed she can, though," interposed Mrs. Stuart, halting in one of her gracious sweeps down the room with her husband's private secretary.

"Don't shout so, captain. I can hear every sentence you uttah—of course Mrs. McDonald can wear blue—she has a morning gown of cadet blue that she is a picture in."

"You are both very kind," said Christie. "I like blue; it is the color of all the Hudson's Bay posts, and the factor's residence is always decorated in blue."

"Is it really? How interesting—do tell us some more of your old home, Mrs. McDonald; you so seldom speak of your life at the post, and we fellows so often wish to hear of it all," said Logan eagerly.

"Why do you not ask me of it, then?"

"Well—er, I'm sure I don't know; I'm fully interested in the Ind—in your people—your mother's people, I mean, but it always seems so personal, I suppose; and—a—a—"

"Perhaps you are, like all other white people, afraid to mention my nationality to me."

The captain winced, and Mrs. Stuart laughed uneasily. Joe McDonald was not far off, and he was listening, and chuckling, and saying to himself, "That's you, Christie, lay 'em out; it won't hurt 'em to know how they appear once in a while."

"Well, Captain Logan," she was saying, "what is it you would like to hear—of my people, or my parents, or myself?"

"All, all, my dear," cried Mrs. Stuart clamorously. "I'll speak for him—tell us of yourself and your mother—your father is delightful, I am sure—but then he is only an ordinary Englishman, not half as interesting as a foreigner, or—or, perhaps I should say, a native."

Christie laughed. "Yes," she said, "my father often teases my mother now about how *very* native she was when he married her; then, how could she have been otherwise? She did not know a word of English, and there was not another English-speaking person besides my father and his two companions within sixty miles."

"Two companions, eh? one a Catholic priest and the other a wine merchant, I suppose, and with your father in the Hudson Bay, they were good representatives of the pioneers in the New World," remarked Logan, waggishly.

"Oh, no, they were all Hudson Bay men. There were no rum-sellers and no missionaries in that part of the country then."

Mrs. Stuart looked puzzled. "*No missionaries?*" she repeated with an odd intonation.

Christie's insight was quick. There was a peculiar expression of interrogation in the eyes of her listeners, and the girl's blood leapt angrily up into her temples as she said hurriedly, "I know what you mean; I know what you are thinking. You are wondering how my parents were married—"

"Well—er, my dear, it seems peculiar—if there was no priest, and no magistrate, why—a—" Mrs. Stuart paused awkwardly.

"The marriage was performed by Indian rites," said Christie.

"Oh, do tell me about it; is the ceremony very interesting and quaint—are your chieftains anything like Buddhist priests?" It was Logan who spoke.

"Why, no," said the girl in amazement at that gentleman's ignorance. "There is no ceremony at all, save a feast. The two people just agree to live only with and for each other, and the man takes his wife to his home, just as you do. There is no ritual to bind them; they need none; an Indian's word was his law in those days, you know."

Mrs. Stuart stepped backwards. "Ah!" was all she said. Logan removed his eye-glass and stared blankly at Christie. "And did McDonald marry you in this singular fashion?" he questioned.

"Oh, no, we were married by Father O'Leary. Why do you ask?"

"Because if he had, I'd have blown his brains out tomorrow."

Mrs. Stuart's partner, who had hitherto been silent, coughed and began to twirl his cuff stud nervously, but nobody took any notice of him. Christie had risen, slowly, ominously—risen, with the dignity and pride of an empress.

"Captain Logan," she said, "what do you dare to say to me? What do you dare to mean? Do you presume to think it would not have been lawful for Charlie to marry me according to my people's rites? Do you for one instant dare to question that my parents were not as legally—"

"Don't, dear, don't," interrupted Mrs. Stuart hurriedly; "it is bad enough now, goodness knows; don't make—" Then she broke off blindly. Christie's eyes glared at the mumbling woman, at her uneasy partner, at the horrified captain. Then they rested on the McDonald brothers, who stood within earshot, Joe's face scarlet, her husband's white as ashes, with something in his eyes she had never seen before. It was Joe who saved the situation. Stepping quickly across towards his sister-in-law, he offered her his arm, saying, "The next dance is ours, I think, Christie."

Then Logan pulled himself together, and attempted to carry Mrs. Stuart off for the waltz, but for once in her life that lady had lost her head. "It is shocking!" she said, "outrageously shocking! I wonder if they told Mr. McDonald before he married her!" Then looking hurriedly round, she too saw the young husband's face—and knew that they had not.

"Humph! deuced nice kettle of fish—and poor old Charlie has always thought so much of honorable birth."

Logan thought he spoke in an undertone, but "poor old Charlie" heard him. He followed his wife and brother across the room. "Joe," he said, "will you see that a trap is called?" Then to Christie, "Joe will see that you get home all right." He wheeled on his heel then and left the ball-room.

Joe *did* see.

He tucked a poor, shivering, pallid little woman into a cab, and wound her bare throat up in the scarlet velvet cloak that was hanging uselessly over her arm. She crouched down beside him, saying, "I am so cold, Joe; I am so cold," but she did not seem to know enough to wrap herself up. Joe felt all through this long drive that nothing this side of Heaven would be so good as to die, and he was glad when the poor little voice at his elbow said, "What is he so angry at, Joe?"

"I don't know exactly, dear," he said gently, "but I think it was what you said about this Indian marriage."

"But why should I not have said it? Is there anything wrong about it?" she asked pitifully.

"Nothing, that I can see—there was no other way; but Charlie is very angry, and you must be brave and forgiving with him, Christie, dear."

"But I did never see him like that before, did you?"

"Once."

"When?"

"Oh, at college, one day, a boy tore his prayer-book in half, and threw it into the grate, just to be mean, you know. Our mother had given it to him at his confirmation."

"And did he look so?"

"About, but it all blew over in a day—Charlie's tempers are short and brisk. Just don't take any notice of him; run off to bed, and he'll have forgotten it by the morning."

They reached home at last. Christie said goodnight quietly, going directly to her room. Joe went to his room also, filled a pipe and smoked for an hour. Across the passage he could hear her slippered feet pacing up and down, up and down the length of her apartment. There was something panther-like in those restless footfalls, a meaning velvetyness that made him shiver, and again he wished he were dead—or elsewhere.

After a time the hall door opened, and someone came upstairs, along the passage, and to the little woman's room. As he entered, she turned and faced him.

"Christie," he said harshly, "do you know what you have done?"

"Yes," taking a step nearer him, her whole soul springing up into her eyes, "I have angered you, Charlie, and—"

"Angered me? You have disgraced me; and, moreover, you have disgraced yourself and both your parents."

"*Disgraced?*"

"Yes, *disgraced*; you have literally declared to the whole city that your father and mother were never married, and that you are the child of—what shall we call it—love? certainly not legality."

Across the hallway sat Joe McDonald, his blood freezing; but it leapt into every vein like fire at the awful anguish in the little voice that cried simply, "Oh! Charlie!"

"How could you do it, how could you do it, Christie, without shame either for yourself or for me, let alone your parents?"

The voice was like an angry demon's—not a trace was there in it of the yellow-haired, blue-eyed, laughing-lipped boy who had driven away so gaily to the dance five hours before.

"Shame? Why should I be ashamed of the rites of my people any more than you should be ashamed of the customs of yours— of a marriage more sacred and holy than half of your white man's mockeries."

It was the voice of another nature in the girl—the love and the pleading were dead in it.

"Do you mean to tell me, Charlie—you who have studied my race and their laws for years—do you mean to tell me that, because there was no priest and no magistrate, my mother was not married? Do you mean to say that all my forefathers, for hundreds of years back, have been illegally born? If so, you blacken my ancestry beyond—beyond—beyond all reason."

"No, Christie, I would not be so brutal as that; but your father and mother live in more civilized times. Father O'Leary has been at the post for nearly twenty years. Why was not your father straight enough to have the ceremony performed when he *did* get the chance?"

The girl turned upon him with the face of a fury. "Do you suppose," she almost hissed, "that my mother would be married according to your *white* rites after she had been five years a wife, and I had been born in the meantime? *No*, a thousand times I say, *no*. When the priest came with his notions of Christianizing, and talked to them of re-marriage by the Church, my mother arose and said, "Never—never—I have never had but this one husband; he has had none but me for wife, and to have you re-marry us would be to say as much to the whole world as that we had never been married before. You go away; *I* do not ask that *your* people be re-married; talk not so to me. I *am* married, and you or the Church cannot do or undo it."

"Your father was a fool not to insist upon the law, and so was the priest."

"Law? *My* people have *no* priest, and my nation cringes not to law. Our priest is purity, and our law is honor. Priest? Was there a *priest* at the most holy marriage known to humanity—that stainless marriage whose offspring is the God you white men told my pagan mother of?"

"Christie—you are *worse* than blasphemous; such a profane remark shows how little you understand the sanctity of the Christian faith—"

"I know what I *do* understand; it is that you are hating me because I told some of the beautiful customs of my people to Mrs. Stuart and those men."

"Pooh! who cares for them? It is not them; the trouble is they won't keep their mouths shut. Logan's a cad and will toss the whole tale about at the club before to-morrow night; and as for the Stuart woman, I'd like to know how I'm going to take you to Ottawa for presentation and the opening, while she is blabbing the whole miserable scandal in every drawing-room, and I'll be pointed out as a romantic fool, and you—as worse; I *can't* understand why your father didn't tell me before we were married; I at least might have warned you to never mention it." Something of recklessness rang up through his voice, just as the panther-likeness crept up from her footsteps and couched herself in hers. She spoke in tones quiet, soft, deadly.

"Before we were married! Oh! Charlie, would it have—made—any—difference?"

"God knows," he said, throwing himself into a chair, his blonde hair rumpled and wet. It was the only boyish thing about him now.

She walked towards him, then halted in the centre of the room. "Charlie McDonald," she said, and it was as if a stone had spoken, "look up." He raised his head, startled by her tone. There was a threat in her eyes that, had his rage been less courageous, his pride less bitterly wounded, would have cowed him.

"There was no such time as that before our marriage, for we *are not married now*. Stop," she said, outstretching her palms against him as he sprang to his feet, "I tell you we are not married. Why should I recognize the rites of your nation when you do not acknowledge the rites of mine? According to your own words, my parents should have gone through your church ceremony as well as through an Indian contract; according to *my* words, *we* should go through an Indian contract as well as through a church marriage. If their union is illegal, so is ours. If you think my father is living in dishonor with my mother, my people will think I am living in dishonor with you. How do I know when another nation will come and conquer you as you white men conquered us? And they will have another marriage rite to perform, and they will tell us another truth, that you are not my husband, that you are but disgracing and dishonoring me, that you are keeping me here, not as your wife, but as your—your—*squaw*."

The terrible word had never passed her lips before, and the blood stained her face to her very temples. She snatched off her wedding ring and tossed it across the room, saying scornfully, "That thing is as empty to me as the Indian rites to you."

He caught her by the wrists; his small white teeth were locked tightly, his blue eyes blazed into hers.

"Christine, do you dare to doubt my honor towards you? *you*, whom I should have died for; do you *dare* to think I have kept you here, not as my wife, but—"

"Oh, God! You are hurting me; you are breaking my arm," she gasped.

The door was flung open, and Joe McDonald's sinewy hands clinched like vices on his brother's shoulders.

"Charlie, you're mad, mad as the devil. Let go of her this minute."

The girl staggered backwards as the iron fingers loosed her wrists. "Oh! Joe," she cried, "I am not his wife, and he says I am born—nameless."

"Here," said Joe, shoving his brother towards the door. "Go downstairs till you can collect your senses. If ever a being acted like an infernal fool, you're the man."

The young husband looked from one to the other, dazed by his wife's insult, abandoned to a fit of ridiculously childish temper. Blind as he was with passion, he remembered long afterwards seeing them standing there, his brother's face darkened with a scowl of anger—his wife, clad in the mockery of her ball dress, her scarlet velvet cloak half covering her bare brown neck and arms, her eyes like flames of fire, her face like a piece of sculptured graystone.

Without a word he flung himself furiously from the room, and immediately afterwards they heard the heavy hall door bang behind him.

"Can I do anything for you, Christie?" asked her brother-in-law calmly.

"No, thank you—unless—I think I would like a drink of water, please."

He brought her up a goblet filled with wine; her hand did not even tremble as she took it. As for Joe, a demon arose in his soul as he noticed she kept her wrists covered.

"Do you think he will come back?" she said.

"Oh, yes, of course; he'll be all right in the morning. Now go to bed like a good little girl, and—and, I say, Christie, you can call me if you want anything; I'll be right here, you know."

"Thank you, Joe; you are kind—and good."

He returned then to his apartment. His pipe was out, but he picked up a newspaper instead, threw himself into an armchair, and in a half-hour was in the land of dreams.

When Charlie came home in the morning, after a six-mile walk into the country and back again, his foolish anger was dead and buried. Logan's "Poor old Charlie" did not ring so distinctly in his ears. Mrs. Stuart's horrified expression had faded considerably from his recollection. He thought only of that surprisingly tall, dark girl, whose eyes looked like coals, whose voice pierced him like a flint-tipped arrow. Ah, well, they would never quarrel again like that, he told himself. She loved him so, and would forgive him after he had talked quietly to her, and told her what an ass he was. She was simple-minded and awfully ignorant to pitch those old Indian laws at him in her fury, but he could not blame her; oh, no, he could not for one moment blame her. He had been terribly severe and un-reasonable, and the horrid McDonald temper had got the better of him; and he loved her so. Oh! he loved her so! She would surely feel that, and forgive him, and— He went straight to his wife's room. The blue velvet evening dress lay on the chair into which he had thrown himself when he doomed his life's happiness by those two words, "God knows." A bunch of dead daffodils and her slippers were on the floor, everything—but Christie.

He went to his brother's bedroom door.

"Joe," he called, rapping nervously thereon; "Joe, wake up; where's Christie, d'you know?"

"Good Lord, no," gasped that youth, springing out of his arm-chair and opening the door. As he did so a note fell from off the handle. Charlie's face blanched to his very hair while Joe read aloud, his voice weakening at every word:—

"Dear Old Joe,—I went into your room at daylight to get that picture of the Post on your bookshelves. I hope you do not mind, but I kissed your hair while you slept; it was so curly, and yellow, and soft, just like his. Good-bye, Joe.

"Christie."

And when Joe looked into his brother's face and saw the anguish settle in those laughing blue eyes, the despair that drove the dimples away from that almost girlish mouth; when he realized that this boy was but four-and-twenty years old, and that all his future was perhaps darkened and shadowed for ever, a great, deep sorrow arose in his heart, and he forgot all things, all but the agony that rang up through the voice of the fair, handsome lad as he staggered forward, crying, "Oh! Joe—what shall I do—what shall I do!"

It was months and months before he found her, but during all that time he had never known a hopeless moment; discouraged he often was, but despondent, never. The sunniness of his ever-boyish heart radiated with a warmth that would have flooded a much deeper gloom than that which settled within his eager young life. Suffer? ah! yes, he suffered, not with locked teeth and stony stoicism, not with the masterful self-command, the reserve, the conquered bitterness of the still-water sort of nature, that is supposed to run to such depths. He tried to be bright, and his sweet old boyish self. He would laugh sometimes in a pitiful, pathetic fashion. He took to petting dogs, looking into their large, solemn eyes with his wistful, questioning blue ones; he would kiss them, as women sometimes do, and call them "dear old fellow," in tones that had tears; and once in the course of his travels, while at a little way-station, he discovered a huge St. Bernard imprisoned by some mischance in an empty freight car; the animal was nearly dead from starvation, and it seemed to salve his own sick heart to rescue back the dog's life. Nobody claimed the big starving creature, the train hands knew nothing of its owner, and gladly handed it over to its deliverer. "Hudson," he called it, and afterwards when Joe McDonald would relate the story of his brother's life he invariably terminated it with, "And I really believe that big lumbering brute saved him." From what, he was never known to say.

But all things end, and he heard of her at last. She had never returned to the Post, as he at first thought she would, but had gone to the little town of B——, in Ontario, where she was making her living at embroidery and plain sewing.

The September sun had set redly when at last he reached the outskirts of the town, opened up the wicket gate, and walked up the weedy, unkept path leading to the cottage where she lodged.

Even through the twilight, he could see her there, leaning on the rail of the verandah—oddly enough she had about her shoulders the scarlet velvet cloak she wore when he had flung himself so madly from the room that night.

The moment the lad saw her his heart swelled with a sudden heat, burning moisture leapt into his eyes, and clogged his long, boyish lashes. He bounded up the steps—"Christie," he said, and the word scorched his lips like audible flame.

She turned to him, and for a second stood magnetized by his passionately wistful face; her peculiar grayish eyes seemed to drink the very life of his unquenchable love, though the tears that suddenly sprang into his seemed to absorb every pulse in his body through those hungry, pleading eyes of his that had, oh! so often been blinded by her kisses when once her whole world lay in their blue depths.

"You will come back to me, Christie, my wife? My wife, you will let me love you again?"

She gave a singular little gasp, and shook her head. "Don't, oh! don't," he cried piteously. "You will come to me, dear? it is all such a bitter mistake—I did not understand. Oh! Christie, I did not understand, and you'll forgive me, and love me again, won't you—won't you?"

"No," said the girl with quick, indrawn breath.

He dashed the back of his hand across his wet eyelids. His lips were growing numb, and he bungled over the monosyllable "Why?"

"I do not like you," she answered quietly.

"God! Oh! God, what is there left?"

She did not appear to hear the heart-break in his voice; she stood like one wrapped in sombre thought; no blaze, no tear, nothing in her eyes; no hardness, no tenderness about her mouth. The wind was blowing her cloak aside, and the only visible human life in her whole body was once when he spoke the muscles of her brown arm seemed to contract.

"But, darling, you are mine—*mine*—we are husband and wife! Oh, heaven, you *must* love me, you *must* come to me again."

"You cannot *make* me come," said the icy voice, "neither church, nor law, nor even"—and the voice softened—"nor even love can make a slave of a red girl."

"Heaven forbid it," he faltered. "No, Christie, I will never claim you without your love. What reunion would that be? But oh, Christie, you are lying to me, you are lying to yourself, you are lying to heaven."

She did not move. If only he could touch her he felt as sure of her yielding as he felt sure there was a hereafter. The memory of times when he had but to lay his hand on her hair to call a most passionate response from her filled his heart with a torture that choked all words before they reached his lips; at the thought of those days he forgot she was unapproachable, forgot how forbidding were her eyes, how stony her lips. Flinging himself forward, his knee on the chair at her side, his face pressed hardly in the folds of the cloak on her shoulder, he clasped his arms about her with a boyish petulance, saying, "Christie, Christie, my little girl wife, I love you, I love you, and you are killing me."

She quivered from head to foot as his fair, wavy hair brushed her neck, his despairing face sank lower until his cheek, hot as fire, rested on the cool, olive flesh of her arm. A warm moisture oozed up through her skin, and as he felt its glow he looked up. Her teeth, white and cold, were locked over her under lip, and her eyes were as gray stones.

Not murderers alone know the agony of a death sentence.

"Is it all useless? all useless, dear?" he said, with lips starving for hers.

"All useless," she repeated. "I have no love for you now. You forfeited me and my heart months ago, when you said *those two words*."

His arms fell away from her wearily, he arose mechanically, he placed his little gray checked cap on the back of his yellow curls, the old-time laughter was dead in the blue eyes that now looked scared and haunted, the boyishness and the dimples crept away for ever from the lips that quivered like a child's; he turned from her, but she had looked once into his face as the Law Giver must have looked at the land of Canaan outspread at his feet. She watched him go down the long path and through the picket gate, she watched the big yellowish dog that had waited for him lumber up on to its feet —stretch—then follow him. She was conscious of but two things, the vengeful lie in her soul, and a little space on her arm that his wet lashes had brushed.

It was hours afterwards when he reached his room. He had said nothing, done nothing—what use were words or deeds? Old Jimmy Robinson was right; she had "balked" sure enough.

What a bare, hotelish room it was! He tossed off his coat and sat for ten minutes looking blankly at the sputtering gas jet. Then his whole life, desolate as a desert, loomed up before him with appalling distinctness. Throwing himself on the floor beside his bed, with clasped hands and arms outstretched on the white counterpane, he sobbed. "Oh! God, dear God, I thought you loved me; I thought you'd let me have her again, but you must be tired of me, tired of loving me too. I've nothing left now, nothing! it doesn't seem that I even have you tonight."

He lifted his face then, for his dog, big and clumsy and yellow, was licking at his sleeve.

The Tenas Klootchman*

PAULINE JOHNSON

This story came to me from the lips of Maarda herself. It was hard to realize, while looking at her placid and happy face, that Maarda had ever been a mother of sorrows, but the healing of a wounded heart oftentimes leaves a light like that of a benediction on a receptive face, and Maarda's countenance held something greater than beauty, something more like lovableness, than any other quality.

We sat together on the deck of the little steamer throughout the long violet twilight, that seems loath to leave the channels and rocky shores of the Upper Pacific in June time. We had dropped easily into conversation, for nothing so readily helps one to an introduction as does the friendly atmosphere of the extreme West, and I had paved the way by greeting her in the Chinook, to which she responded with a sincere and friendly handclasp.

Dinner on the small coast-wise steamers is almost a function. It is the turning-point of the day, and is served English fashion, in the evening. The passengers "dress" a little for it, eat the meal leisurely and with relish. People who perhaps have exchanged no conversation during the day, now relax, and fraternize with their fellow men and women.

I purposely secured a seat at the dining-table beside Maarda. Even she had gone through a simple "dressing" for dinner, having smoothed her satiny black hair, knotted a brilliant silk handkerchief about her throat, and laid aside her large, heavy plaid shawl, revealing a fine delaine gown of green, bordered with two flat rows of black silk velvet ribbon. That silk velvet ribbon, and the fashion in which it was applied, would have bespoken her nationality, even had her dark copper-colored face failed to do so.

*In the Chinook language, "Tenas Klootchman" means "girl baby."

35

The average Indian woman adores silk and velvet, and will have none of cotton, and these decorations must be in symmetrical rows, not designs. She holds that the fabric is in itself excellent enough. Why twist it and cut it into figures that would only make it less lovely?

We chatted a little during dinner. Maarda told me that she and her husband lived at the Squamish River, some thirty-five miles north of Vancouver City, but when I asked if they had any children, she did not reply, but almost instantly called my attention to a passing vessel seen through the porthole. I took the hint, and said no more of family matters, but talked of the fishing and the prospects of a good sockeye run this season.

Afterwards, however, while I stood alone on deck watching the sun set over the rim of the Pacific, I felt a feathery touch on my arm. I turned to see Maarda, once more enveloped in her shawl, and holding two deck stools. She beckoned with a quick uplift of her chin, and said, "We'll sit together here, with no one about us, and I'll tell you of the child." And this was her story:

She was the most beautiful little Tenas Klootchman a mother could wish for, bright, laughing, pretty as a spring flower, but— just as frail. Such tiny hands, such buds of feet! One felt that they must never take her out of her cradle basket for fear that, like a flower stem, she would snap asunder and her little head droop like a blossom.

But Maarda's skilful fingers had woven and plaited and colored the daintiest cradle basket in the entire river district for this little woodland daughter. She had fished long and late with her husband, so that the canner's money would purchase silk "blankets" to en-wrap her treasure; she had beaded cradle bands to strap the wee body securely in its cosy resting-nest. Ah, it was such a basket, fit for an English princess to sleep in! Everything about it was fine, soft, delicate, and everything born of her mother-love.

So, for weeks, for even months, the little Tenas Klootchman laughed and smiled, waked and slept, dreamed and dimpled in her pretty playhouse. Then one day, in the hot, dry summer, there was no smile. The dimples did not play. The little flower paled, the small face grew smaller, the tiny hands tinier; and one morning, when the birds awoke in the forests of the Squamish, the eyes of the little Tenas Klootchman remained closed.

They put her to sleep under the giant cedars, the lulling, singing firs, the whispering pines that must now be her lullaby, instead of her mother's voice crooning the child-songs of the Pacific, that tell of baby foxes and gamboling baby wolves and bright-eyed baby birds. Nothing remained to Maarda but an empty little cradle basket, but smoothly-folded silken "blankets," but disused beaded bands. Often at nightfall she would stand alone, and watch the sun dip into the far waters, leaving the world as grey and colorless as her own life; she would outstretch her arms—pitifully empty arms—towards the west, and beneath her voice again croon the lullabies of the Pacific, telling of the baby foxes, the soft, furry baby wolves, and the little downy fledglings in the nests. Once in an agony of loneliness she sang these things aloud, but her husband heard her, and his face turned grey and drawn, and her soul told her she must not be heard again singing these things aloud.

And one evening a little steamer came into harbor. Many Indians came ashore from it, as the fishing season had begun. Among others was a young woman over whose face the finger of illness had traced shadows and lines of suffering. In her arms she held a baby, a beautiful, chubby, round-faced, healthy child that seemed too heavy for her wasted form to support. She looked about her wistfully, evidently seeking a face that was not there, and as the steamer pulled out of the harbor, she sat down weakly on the wharf, laid the child across her lap, and buried her face in her hands. Maarda touched her shoulder.

"Who do you look for?" she asked.

"For my brother Luke 'Alaska,'" replied the woman. "I am ill, my husband is dead, my brother will take care of me; he's a good man."

"Luke 'Alaska,'" said Maarda. What had she heard of Luke "Alaska"? Why, of course, he was one of the men her own husband had taken a hundred miles up the coast as axeman on a surveying party, but she dared not tell this sick woman. She only said: "You had better come with me. My husband is away, but in a day or two he will be able to get news to your brother. I'll take care of you till they come."

The woman arose gratefully, then swayed unsteadily under the weight of the child. Maarda's arms were flung out, yearningly, longingly, towards the baby.

"Where is your cradle basket to carry him in?" she asked, looking about among the boxes and bales of merchandise the steamer had left on the wharf.

"I have no cradle basket. I was too weak to make one, too poor to buy one. I have *nothing*," said the woman.

"Then let me carry him," said Maarda. "It's quite a walk to my place; he's too heavy for you."

The woman yielded the child gratefully, saying, "It's not a boy, but a Tenas Klootchman."

Maarda could hardly believe her senses. That splendid, sturdy, plump, big baby a Tenas Klootchman! For a moment her heart surged with bitterness. Why had her own little girl been so frail, so flower-like? But with the touch of that warm baby body, the bitterness faded. She walked slowly, fitting her steps to those of the sick woman, and jealously lengthening the time wherein she could hold and hug the baby in her yearning arms.

The woman was almost exhausted when they reached Maarda's home, but strong tea and hot, wholesome food revived her; but fever burned brightly in her cheeks and eyes. The woman was very ill, extremely ill. Maarda said, "You must go to bed, and as soon as you are there, I will take the canoe and go for a doctor. It is two or three miles, but you stay resting, and I'll bring him. We will put the Tenas Klootchman beside you in—" she hesitated. Her glance travelled up to the wall above, where a beautiful empty cradle basket hung, with folded silken "blankets" and disused beaded bands.

The woman's gaze followed hers, a light of beautiful understanding pierced the fever glare of her eyes, she stretched out her hot hand protestingly, and said, "Don't put her in—that. Keep that, it is yours. She is used to being rolled only in my shawl."

But Maarda had already lifted the basket down, and was tenderly arranging the wrappings. Suddenly her hands halted, she seemed to see a wee flower face looking up to her like the blossom of a russet-brown pansy. She turned abruptly, and, going to the door, looked out speechlessly on the stretch of sea and sky glimmering through the tree trunks.

For a time she stood. Then across the silence broke the little murmuring sound of a baby half crooning, half crying, indoors, the little cradleless baby that, homeless, had entered her home. Maarda returned, and, lifting the basket, again arranged the wrappings. "The Tenas Klootchman shall have this cradle," she said, gently. The sick woman turned her face to the wall and sobbed.

It was growing dark when Maarda left her guests, and entered her canoe on the quest for a doctor. The clouds hung low, and a fine, slanting rain fell, from which she protected herself as best she could with a shawl about her shoulders, crossed in front, with each end tucked into her belt beneath her arms—Indian-fashion. Around rocks and boulders, headlands and crags, she paddled, her little craft riding the waves like a cork, but pitching and plunging with every stroke. By and by the wind veered, and blew head on, and now and again she shipped water; her skirts began dragging heavily about her wet ankles, and her moccasins were drenched. The wind increased, and she discarded her shawl to afford greater freedom to her arm-play. The rain drove and slanted across her shoulders and head, and her thick hair was dripping with sea moisture and the downpour.

Sometimes she thought of beaching the canoe and seeking shelter until daylight. Then she again saw those fever-haunted eyes of the stranger who was within her gates, again heard the half wail of the Tenas Klootchman in her own baby's cradle basket, and at the sound she turned her back on the possible safety of shelter, and forged ahead.

It was a wearied woman who finally knocked at the doctor's door and bade him hasten. But his strong man's arm found the return journey comparatively easy paddling. The wind helped him, and Maarda also plied her bow paddle, frequently urging him to hasten.

It was dawn when they entered her home. The sick woman moaned, and the child fretted for food. The doctor bent above his patient, shaking his head ruefully as Maarda built the fire, and attended to the child's needs before she gave thought to changing her drenched garments. All day she attended her charges, cooked, toiled, watched, forgetting her night of storm and sleeplessness in the greater anxieties of ministering to others. The doctor came and went between her home and the village, but always with that solemn headshake, that spoke so much more forcibly than words.

"She shall not die!" declared Maarda. "The Tenas Klootchman needs her, she shall not die!" But the woman grew feebler daily, her eyes grew brighter, her cheeks burned with deeper scarlet.

"We must fight for it now," said the doctor. And Maarda and he fought the dread enemy hour after hour, day after day.

Bereft of its mother's care, the Tenas Klootchman turned to Maarda, laughed to her, crowed to her, until her lonely heart embraced the child as a still evening embraces a tempestuous day. Once she had a long, terrible fight with herself. She had begun to feel her ownership in the little thing, had begun to regard it as her right to tend and pet it. Her heart called out for it; and she wanted it for her very own. She began to feel a savage, tigerish joy in thinking —aye, *knowing* that it really would belong to her and to her alone soon—very soon.

When this sensation first revealed itself to her, the doctor was there—had even told her the woman could not recover. Maarda's gloriously womanly soul was horrified at itself. She left the doctor in charge, and went to the shore, fighting out this outrageous gladness, strangling it—killing it.

She returned, a sanctified being, with every faculty in her body, every sympathy of her heart, every energy of her mind devoted to bringing this woman back from the jaws of death. She greeted the end of it all with a sorrowing, half-breaking heart, for she had learned to love the woman she had envied, and to weep for the little child who lay so helplessly against her unselfish heart.

A beautifully lucid half-hour came to the fever-stricken one just before the Call to the Great Beyond!

"Maarda," she said, "you have been a good Tillicum to me, and I can give you nothing for all your care, your kindness—unless—" Her eyes wandered to her child peacefully sleeping in the delicately-woven basket. Maarda saw the look, her heart leaped with a great joy. Did the woman wish to give the child to her? She dared not ask for it. Suppose Luke "Alaska" wanted it. His wife loved children, though she had four of her own in their home far inland. Then the sick woman spoke:

"Your cradle basket and your heart were empty before I came. Will you keep my Tenas Klootchman as your own?—to fill them both again?"

Maarda promised. "Mine was a Tenas Klootchman, too," she said.

"Then I will go to her, and be her mother, wherever she is, in the Spirit Islands they tell us of," said the woman. "We will be but exchanging our babies, after all."

When morning dawned, the woman did not awake.

Maarda had finished her story, but the recollections had saddened her eyes, and for a time we both sat on the deck in the violet twilight without exchanging a word.

"Then the little Tenas Klootchman is yours now?" I asked.

A sudden radiance suffused her face, all trace of melancholy vanished. She fairly scintillated happiness.

"Mine!" she said. "All mine! Luke 'Alaska' and his wife said she was more mine than theirs, that I must keep her as my own. My husband rejoiced to see the cradle basket filled, and to hear me laugh as I used to."

"How I should like to see the baby!" I began.

"You shall," she interrupted. Then with a proud, half-roguish expression, she added:

"She is so strong, so well, so heavy; she sleeps a great deal, and wakes laughing and hungry."

As night fell, an ancient Indian woman came up the companion-way. In her arms she carried a beautifully-woven basket cradle, within which nestled a round-cheeked, smiling-eyed baby. Across its little forehead hung locks of black, straight hair, and its sturdy limbs were vainly endeavoring to free themselves from the lacing of the "blankets." Maarda took the basket, with an expression on her face that was transfiguring.

"Yes, this is my little Tenas Klootchman," she said, as she unlaced the bands, then lifted the plump little creature out on to her lap.

Soon afterwards the steamer touched an obscure little harbor, and Maarda, who was to join her husband there, left me, with a happy good-night. As she was going below, she faltered, and turned back to me. "I think sometimes," she said, quietly, "the Great Spirit thought my baby would feel motherless in the far Spirit Islands, so He gave her the woman I nursed for a mother; and He knew I was childless, and He gave me this child for my daughter. Do you think I am right? Do you understand?"

"Yes," I said, "I think you are right, and I understand."

Once more she smiled radiantly, and turning, descended the companionway. I caught a last glimpse of her on the wharf. She was greeting her husband, her face a mirror of happiness. About the delicately-woven basket cradle she had half pulled her heavy plaid shawl, beneath which the two rows of black velvet ribbon bordering her skirt proclaimed once more her nationality.

Angel DeCora

Angel DeCora was born on May 3, 1871, on the Winnebago Reservation in Nebraska. Her father, David DeCora, was of French-Winnebago ancestry, and her mother was a member of the La Mere family. Her Winnebago name, which she often used as a pen name, was Hinookmahiwi-kilinaka (Woman Coming on the Cloud in Glory).

Angel DeCora first attended reservation school and afterward was sent to the Hampton Institute, where she graduated in 1891. She continued her education at the Burnham Classical School for Girls in Massachusetts and then enrolled for a four-year course in the Smith College art department. Later she transferred to the Drexel Institute, where she came under the tutelage of illustrator Howard Pyle. He arranged for her to perfect her artistic skills for another two years at the Boston Museum of Fine Arts School.

Following completion of her academic training, Angel DeCora set up a private studio in New York City and established a fair reputation as a book illustrator, working on such books as Francis La Flesche's *The Middle Five* (1900), Gertrude Bonnin's *American Indian Legends* (1901), Natalie Curtis's *The Indian's Book* (1907), and Elaine Goodale Eastman's *Yellow Star* (1911). While preparing the illustrations for *American Indian Legends*, she struck up what would become a lasting friendship with Gertrude Bonnin.

In 1906 she became the head of the art department at the Carlisle Indian school, a position she held for nine years. There she developed an intensive art program for Indian students, encouraging them to apply Indian designs to modern art media. At Carlisle she also met and later married Sioux artist William Dietz.

Angel DeCora lectured widely on the subject of Indian affairs and was an active member of the Society of American Indians. She

43

also wrote a number of articles, including several on Indian art, two autobiographical sketches, and the story included here, which may be autobiographical.

At the outbreak of World War I DeCora obtained a position at the New York State Museum in Albany, and after her divorce in 1918 she returned to New York to continue her illustrating work. She died there on February 6, 1919.

REFERENCES

Curtis, Natalie. "An American Indian Artist." *Outlook*, January 14, 1920, 64–66.
DeCora, Angel. "An Autobiography." *Red Man*, March 1911, 279–285.
Dockstader, Frederick J. *Great North American Indians*. New York: Van Nostrand, 1977.
Eastman, Elaine G. "In Memoriam: Angel DeCora Dietz." *American Indian Magazine* 7 (Spring 1919): 51–52.

STORY BY ANGEL DECORA

"The Sick Child." *Harper's Monthly*, February 1899, 446–448.

The Sick Child

HENOOK-MAKHEWE-KELENAKA

[ANGEL DECORA]

It was about sunset when I, a little child, was sent with a handful of powdered tobacco leaves and red feathers to make an offering to the spirit who had caused the sickness of my little sister. It had been a long, hard winter, and the snow lay deep on the prairie as far as the eye could reach. The medicine-woman's directions had been that the offering must be laid upon the naked earth, and that to find it I must face toward the setting sun.

I was taught the prayer: "Spirit grandfather, I offer this to thee. I pray thee restore my little sister to health." Full of reverence and a strong faith that I could appease the anger of the spirit, I started out to plead for the life of our little one.

But now where was a spot of earth to be found in all that white monotony? They had talked of death at the house. I hoped that my little sister would live, but I was afraid of nature.

I reached a little spring. I looked down to its pebbly bottom, wondering whether I should leave my offering there, or keep on in search of a spot of earth. If I put my offering in the water, would it reach the bottom and touch the earth, or would it float away, as it had always done when I made my offering to the water spirit?

Once more I started on in my search of the bare ground.

The surface was crusted in some places, and walking was easy; in other places I would wade through a foot or more of snow. Often I paused, thinking to clear the snow away in some place and there lay my offering. But no, my faith must be in nature, and I must trust to it to lay bare the earth.

It was a hard struggle for so small a child.

I went on and on; the reeds were waving their tasselled ends in the wind. I stopped and looked at them. A reed, whirling in the wind, had formed a space round its stem, making a loose socket.

45

I stood looking into the opening. The reed must be rooted in the ground, and the hole must follow the stem to the earth. If I poured my offerings into the hole, surely they must reach the ground; so I said the prayer I had been taught, and dropped my tobacco and red feathers into the opening that nature itself had created.

No sooner was the sacrifice accomplished than a feeling of doubt and fear thrilled me. What if my offering should never reach the earth? Would my little sister die?

Not till I turned homeward did I realize how cold I was. When at last I reached the house they took me in and warmed me, but did not question me, and I said nothing. Everyone was sad, for the little one had grown worse.

The next day the medicine-woman said my little sister was beyond hope; she could not live. Then bitter remorse was mine, for I thought I had been unfaithful, and therefore my little sister was to be called to the spirit-land. I was a silent child, and did not utter my feelings; my remorse was intense.

My parents would not listen to what the medicine-woman had said, but clung to hope. As soon as she had gone, they sent for a medicine-man who lived many miles away.

He arrived about dark. He was a large man, with a sad, gentle face. His presence had always filled me with awe, and that night it was especially so, for he was coming as a holy man. He entered the room where the baby lay, and took a seat, hardly noticing anyone. There was silence saving only for the tinkling of the little tin ornaments on his medicine-bag. He began to speak: "A soul has departed from this house, gone to the spirit-land. As I came I saw luminous vapor above the house. It ascended, it grew less, it was gone on its way to the spirit-land. It was the spirit of the little child who is sick; she still breathes, but her spirit is beyond our reach. If medicine will ease her pain, I will do what I can."

He stood up and blessed the four corners of the earth with song. Then, according to the usual custom of medicine-doctors, he began reciting the vision that had given him the right to be a medicine-man. The ruling force of the vision had been in the form of a bear. To it he addressed his prayer, saying: "Inasmuch as thou hast given me power to cure the sick, and in one case allowing me to unite spirit and body again, if thou seest fit, allow me to recall the spirit of this child to its body once more." He asked that the coverings be taken off the baby, and that it be brought into the middle of the room. Then, as he sang, he danced slowly around the little form. When the song was finished, he blessed the child, and then prepared the medicine, stirring into water some ground herbs. This he took into his mouth and sprinkled it over the little body. Another mixture he gave her to drink.

Almost instantly there was a change; the little one began to breathe more easily, and as the night wore on she seemed to suffer less. Finally she opened her eyes, looked into mother's face, and smiled. The medicine-man, seeing it, said that the end was near, and though he gave her more medicine, the spirit, he said, would never return.

After saying words of comfort, he took his departure, refusing to take a pony and some blankets that were offered him, saying that he had been unable to hold the spirit back, and had no right to accept the gifts.

The next morning I found the room all cleared away, and my mother sat sewing on a little white gown. The bright red trimming caught my eye. I came to her and asked, "Please mother, tell me for whom is that, and why do you make it so pretty?" She made no answer, but bent over her work. I leaned forward that I might look into her face and repeat my question. I bent down, and, oh! the tears were falling fast down her cheeks. Then we were told that our little sister was gone to the spirit-land, and we must not talk about her. They made us look upon her. We felt of her and kissed her, but she made no response. Then I realized what death meant. Remorse again seized me, but I was silent.

William Jones

William Jones was born on March 28, 1871, on the Sac and Fox Reservation in the Indian Territory. His father, Henry Clay Jones, was of Welsh and Fox descent; his mother, Sarah Penny, was an Englishwoman. Because his mother died in childbirth, he was left in the care of his Fox grandmother until the age of nine. He became a member of the Eagle Clan and was given the name Megasiáva (Black Eagle).

At the age of ten, a year after his grandmother died, he was sent to an Indian boarding school maintained by the Society of Friends in Wabash, Indiana (this was probably White's Indiana Manual Labor Institute, which Gertrude Bonnin also attended in 1884). He spent three years there and afterward worked in the Indian Territory as a cowboy. In 1889 he was chosen among other Sac and Fox youths to attend the Hampton Institute, where he was to remain for the next three years. There he became an Episcopalian and learned carpentry.

Jones chose to continue his education and in 1892 enrolled at the Phillips Andover Academy. He graduated in 1896 and then enrolled at Harvard, intending to obtain a degree in medicine. At this time, however, he became acquainted with F. W. Putnam of the Peabody Museum, who stimulated his interest in anthropology. Jones joined the Boston Folklore Society and wrote articles for its *Folk Lore Journal*. In 1897 the organization financed a field trip to the Sac and Fox, after which he made the decision to specialize in North American anthropology. While at Harvard he was twice awarded a Winthrop Scholarship, but to supplement his income he wrote a series of short stories for the *Harvard Monthly* based on his experiences on the range and his fieldwork among the Sac and Fox.

On Putnam's recommendation, he received a scholarship to

Columbia University, where he was awarded a master's degree in 1901 and a doctorate in 1904. His tutor at Columbia was Franz Boas. In preparation for his thesis, he conducted intensive linguistic and ethnological studies among the Sac and Fox under the guidance of the American Museum of Natural History.

Unable to find a means of support that would allow him to continue his work on North American Indians, Jones accepted an offer from the Field Museum in Chicago to conduct an expedition to the Philippines in 1907. There he was ambushed and killed by a group of Ilongots on the island of Luzón on March 29, 1909 (Barbara Stones gives April 2 as the probable date of his death).

Along with Francis La Flesche, Arthur C. Parker, J.N.B. Hewitt, and others, Jones was one of the major Indian anthropologists during the early development of the field in North America. His special area of interest was Algonquian linguistics and oral traditions. His major publications are *Some Principles of Algonquian Word-Formation* (Lancaster, Pa.: New Era Printing Co., 1904); *Fox Texts* (Leyden: E. J. Brill, 1907); *Kickapoo Tales Collected by William Jones*, ed. Truman Michelson (Leyden: E. J. Brill, 1915); and *Ojibwa Texts Collected by William Jones*, ed. Truman Michelson, 2 vols. (Leyden: E. J. Brill, 1917–19).

REFERENCES

Rideaut, H. N., *William Jones*. New York: Frederick A. Stokes Company, 1912.
Stoner, Barbara. "Why Was William Jones Killed?" *Field Museum of Natural History Bulletin* 42 (September 1971): 10–13.

STORIES BY WILLIAM JONES

"An Episode of the Spring Round-Up." *Harvard Monthly* 28 (April 1899): 46–53.
"Anoska Nimiwina." *Harvard Monthly* 28 (May 1899): 102–111.
"Lydie." *Harvard Monthly* 28 (July 1899): 194–201.
"Chiky." *Harvard Monthly* 29 (November 1899): 59–65.

"In the Name of His Ancestor." *Harvard Monthly* 29 (December 1899): 109–115.

"The Usurper of the Range." *Harvard Monthly* 30 (March 1900): 13–22.

"The Heart of the Brave." *Harvard Monthly* 30 (May 1900): 99–106.

"A Lone Star Ranger." *Harvard Monthly* 30 (June 1900): 154–161.

In the Name of His Ancestor

WILLIAM JONES

Tell me, mother, what is keeping my father away so late to-night?

The traps, the beaver traps, my son. You know in these wintry moons when his fur is smooth and soft the beaver can hear from afar the crack of the tiniest twig, can see as far as you, and can scent, oh—I was going to say almost as far as he can see. One of these days you will accompany your father with the traps, and then you will no longer wonder why he has to work so long over them. Come, sit here with me on the buffalo robe before the light of this blaze. Now put your feet close up to the fire, but take care not to burn your moccasins.

Ooh, mother, how the wigwam is shaking! Is Nutenwi, the wind, angry?

Do not fear, my son. But hark, listen to the voices of the trees, our grandparents! It snows, it is growing cold, and the night blackens. Lonely out in the dark stand our grandparents. Now Nutenwi, the wind, is passing among them; and so, bowing together their heads, they are wailing one to another how cold, how lonely, and how sad they are. Their voices are not so full of mirth as in the warm summer moons, when the whip-poor-will, resting upon their shoulders, sings to them songs of the ripening corn.

Hish, listen, my son! Do you hear one moaning out slowly, "Ketona! Ketona!"?

It is Mitwiwa, mother, the old cottonwood down by the spring. I wonder why he should be calling me on a night like this?

Perhaps it is not you he is calling. It may be that the Chipiya, the spirit of the ancestor after whom you are named, is walking forth this night, revisiting the lodges of his people. If so, then it is he old Mitwiwa is calling by name.

Does old Mitwiwa know as much about Ketona as my father? As you, mother?

Yes, and more.

He was the one who long ago—do tell me about him again, will you, mother?

Lay your head down upon my lap then.

You are now eight winters of age. One morning, a moon after you were born, when it was beginning to whiten in the Wabeneki, in the land of the dawn, your father brought Tacumisawa into our wigwam. Tacumisawa, you know, is still the chief of the Eagles, our gens. Shortly after, there came other Eagles, until thirty, perhaps forty, of them were seated in a circle within the lodge. I sat over in a corner among the women and the children, holding you in my lap. After the priests had chanted prayers to Gisha Munetoa, and your father had done serving turkey, venison, and corn to the guests, there fell a silence so quiet in the lodge that we could hear one another breathe. And like the mist that was rising that morning from our brook down there under the hill, lifted the smoke from the long red-stone pipes of the men, floating in slowly whirling rings and in tiny clouds up through the opening in the top of the wigwam. Tacumisawa had long been watching the smoke. By and by he gently laid aside his pipe and, in a tone as low as mine is now, said to us all:

"My brother and my sister Eagles, Gisha Munetoa is looking down upon us. The Eagles who have lived before us are listening. I name this child, Ketona. Hear, and let me tell you why."

And then he went on with the story you have heard over and again from your father. Now all the events of that story happened winters and winters ago in our old Rock River country, far away off in the land of the North. The bitterest foes of our nation then were the Sioux, men of the long nose, hooked like the beak of a hawk. Coming again and again from the country beyond the Mississippi, they tried to drive us away from the Rock River; but finding that they were losing too many scalps, and feeling after each fight that the hearts of our men and of our women were growing stronger and braver, they finally decided that it was better to remain on the western side of the Mississippi.

At sunrise of a morning after the Sioux had been driven over the Great River, four of their men appeared on the bluffs of the eastern bank within sight of our lodges. Even while the runners were yelling the alarm fifteen men had started at the top of their speed toward the bluffs to kill or to capture the hated foe. But when the four Sioux lifted high their left hands, and pressed their right over their hearts, and after the old men down in the village yelled, "Messengers of peace! Messengers of peace! Let them alone! Let them come!" the men halted and unwillingly returned to their lodges. Then the runners went part way out to beckon and to escort the Sioux in.

When the strangers drew near, certain old men met them and shook hands. The Sioux at once asked to meet the chiefs and head men in Council, because they claimed to have had a message of great import from their nation.

Powashik was our chief in those days. After he had called his head men together in his lodge, he sent a runner to fetch in the messengers. When they came and seated themselves by the entrance way, Powashik filled four pipes with sacred tobacco, rolled a live coal into the bowl of each, and then handed a pipe to each of the Sioux. You have seen buzzards sitting on the limb of a tree, how their heads droop, and how still and stiff are their bodies. That was the way the Sioux were sitting as they smoked our sacred pipes, their blankets pulled tightly about their waists and over their shoulders. And when they were done smoking, they rose one after the other and spoke like this:

"Our nation sends us to you with this message: Once upon a time our young men married your young women, and your young men married our young women. We went to war together, and we were friends, close friends. We want to see the days when all these things happened come back again. So let us stop fighting. Winter will soon be here, and neither of us have laid in our buffalo meat. Our messengers will shake hands with you. Shake hands with them, and we will make ready a great feast at our village, two days' journey by canoe up the river. And we would ask you to come to the feast and rejoice with us, because we are once more friends."

Powashik and the old men went out, leaving the Sioux alone in the lodge. Many were so glad at heart that they were for shaking hands with the messengers at once; but some, who in their younger days had won the scalp-lock and eagle feather in wars with the Sioux, shook their heads and counselled against haste. But Powashik was old and gray. He was tired of war. Like most of the old men, he believed in what the Sioux had told him, so he went in and shook hands with them. He told them to say to their nation that his heart was glad, that he wished the things they wished, and that he and many of his head men would go to the feast.

In the morning, the people thronged the shore and the bluffs of the Mississippi to watch Powashik and twenty of his counsellors depart for the village of the Sioux. The old chief and a few of the older men who were weak with the paddle were in their newest buckskins, wore black-tipped eagle feathers on their scalp-locks, and hung beaded and bear-claw necklaces about their necks. They took no war-club, no bow, no arrow, no kind of weapon whatever, because Gisha Munetoa had bade our people long ago never to have these things about them when on a mission of peace. But instead of these things, they had in the canoes tobacco, buckskins, and eagle feathers, all presents of peace to be given to the Sioux at the feast. And the people kept watching the canoes till the last turned the big bend far up the river.

On the evening of the second day before it had begun to grow dark in earnest, Ketona, a young man of twenty winters who had gone to help paddle his father's canoe, was seen coming toward the village. As he drew near, men, women, and children pressed round about him, eager to know about the feast. But when they saw that his leggins and moccasins were torn and spattered with mud, that his naked body and arms had been gashed by thorns and briers, and when they noticed that he hung his head and made no reply, and was making straight for his lodge, they all stopped and gazed after him with mouths wide open. Old men leaning upon their canes crossed fore-fingers over the lips, and, shaking their heads, murmured one to another, "Something bad! Something bad!" As Ketona sat with legs crossed before the fire in his lodge and stared into the flickering blaze with eyes gleaming like those of a panther at bay, his mother stepped softly near, and, fearing she would hear something bad, asked, "My son! My son! What has happened? Why these deep scratches on your body? How came these leggins, these moccasins, to be so yellow with mud?"

Ketona kept looking steadily into the fire, while the eyes of his mother were overflowing with tears. Then she put before him on a mat some dried venison and a wooden bowl with corn in it, and begged:

"Eat, my son. You look tired and hungry. Eat all you want. There is plenty left for your father. Tell me, when will he be home?"

Ketona beckoned his mother to sit down beside him.

"My father," he began in an undertone, "will never come home again. His scalp, and that of old Powashik, and of all who went away yesterday morning, are hanging to-night in the lodges of the Sioux. I am the only one to escape. My heart is too sick to tell you how as we turned in shore last evening to camp, the Sioux pounced upon us as quickly as a hawk upon a dove; how my father yelled to me then, 'Dive, my son! Dive!'; and how, shortly after, when I raised my head above water among the tall reeds under the bank, I saw two men standing proudly over my father's body, one with a tomahawk that had crushed in his skull, the other with a knife that had just taken off his scalp. Do not weep, mother. Be brave. Go tell the people the little I have told you. The rest, they will know later. Tell them not to fear, for the Sioux are far off now on their way to the North into the land of the wild rice. Wait, mother. Give me your right hand. As sure as I am a Red-Earth, as sure as I am an Eagle, and as sure as I am your son, I will see our nation and you and me avenged."

The runners took up the message of the mother and carried it from lodge to lodge. When the women heard it, they gasped, and, for a time, were speechless. By and by, slowly gathering their cloaks about their waists and over their heads, they slipped softly out of the wigwams; and each going to a lonely spot in the forest or on the bluffs of the river, there prayed in silence to Gisha Munetoa. But the men on hearing the news said never a word. Some of them straightened up, clinched their fists, and gritted their teeth.

Two moons had come and gone, and the snow lay deep on the hills, in the valleys, and in the forest. One night Nutenwi, the wind, roared and the snow fell deeper than ever. Even though the snow had banked almost halfway up the lodges, yet in the morning rumor flew through all the village that Ketona and fifty young men were missing, gone no one knew whither. Each of those fifty young men had slipped from his wigwam as a fox from his lair, so that even the nearest kinsman did not know when he had gone. Runners slid over the country far and wide upon snow-shoes, but they could find nowhere the faintest sign of a trail.

That was a bitter winter for our nation. Day and night the women wept, and the men were sick at heart. It was hard enough to lose the old men, but what will become of our nation, they thought, if we must lose our young men, too? But the men and the women were mindful that they were Red-Earth people, and so waited patiently for the day when their young men would return.

And they did return, but not till the snow was melting and the ice was floating in the rivers. Forty of them came home. And the light of day was never so bright as on the afternoon when the forty were seen coming in single file down the bluffs of the river toward the village. And as they came on, men and boys rushed whooping from all the lodges, and, gathering round the young men, accompanied them home. All the while, the women, the girls, and the little children waited in groups before their lodges, their hearts glad, their faces beaming, and all of them proud at seeing long, black scalps dangling like horse-tails from the belts of the young warriors.

In the night a fire was kindled from a pile of logs in front of old Powashik's lodge. The scalp-pole was set up, and on it were hung the scalps of the Sioux. And all around within the firelight sat the men, the women, and the children, all wrapped snugly in blankets. Then back and forth and around the pole danced the young men, stepping to the time of the drum and of the war songs sung by the old warriors. Now and again was a pause in the dance long enough for one to tell a short story of how he had taken a scalp. And when he was done speaking, the chief of his gens amid the whoops of the old warriors stepped up and gave him an eagle feather.

Last of all to speak was Ketona himself. He told how he and the others had slipped into the land of the Sioux, how they had slain warriors and ripped off their scalps before the very eyes of their women, and how they had not let up pursuing the Sioux till they had more than avenged the death of Powashik and that of those slain with him. And when the people saw Ketona standing there in the light of the blaze, holding in his right hand the scalps of the two Sioux who had slain his father, and in the left was holding the knife he had plunged into their hearts and had used to rip off their scalps, they breathed easier and felt that they were beginning to be avenged.

Such, my son, is the story of Ketona as Tacumisawa told it on the morning he gave you your name. And I remember so well when closing he said to us all:

"Now, my brother and my sister Eagles, now that this Eaglet may be brave and do valiant deeds to make him forever remembered by his people, I name him Ketona. And when he is old enough to know this story, this war story of the Eagles, may he wish to be like the Ketona who winters ago leading fifty young braves avenged the death of his father and of the leaders of his nation."

When Tacumisawa was done, your father stepped over to where I was and took you from me. He handed you to Tacumisawa, who stood you on your wabbling legs, your back against his breast. Then rose all the Eagles, the men first; and as they filed past you out of the lodge, they stopped long enough to shake gently this little right hand of yours.

Hish, mother!

Yes, my son, that is the tramp of your father's footstep.

The Heart of the Brave

WILLIAM JONES

Ameno Kisheswa, the moon that summons together the white-tail deer in droves, had been born but a night and a day; and as she hung at twilight in the western sky, she reddened like an up-turned buffalo horn on fire. The flowers, our grandparents, had hushed their glee; and drooping their foreheads, they waited without so much as a whisper of complaint the coming of *Takwaki*, the cruel frost. But the leaves and the grasses were happy, gay in the varied colours of their garments. *Nutenwi*, the big, hollow-mouthed wind, was abroad; and above him, far up, flew quacking geese that strung themselves in lines, bow-like, one after the other, across the heavens, as they journeyed merrily toward the *Shawaneki*, the regions of warmth and sunlight.

It was on a morning of one of these days that Wakamo and a hundred Osakies set out for the Comanche country, the land of plains and home of the buffalo and prairie wolf. Old and young thronged the banks of the Mississippi and watched them paddle across. Women waved and children hallooed as the men in twos, in threes, and in single file passed over the sand bars and disappeared in the shadow of the tall wood beyond. Many of the men were young, only braves. They wore their hair long, letting it fall in two braids each over a shoulder in front. The rest, who had been on a raid before, wore the hair shaved, leaving only a tuft, like that of the blue jay, upon which nodded the feather that marked them off as the warriors. Few were the burdens they took. All were in leggins and moccasins; and over their naked backs were slung the quivers of arrows. In the hand they carried their bows; and at the belt, on the side away from the knife, hung a small bag of dried jerked venison and pounded corn of the season before. At the head of them all, and by the side of the old councillor, Kewanat, went the youthful Wakamo.

The name, Wakamo, only the moon before, had been that of a young man who thought more on the hang of the blanket from his shoulder than on the dangle of a Comanche scalp-lock at his belt. Ever since the day that Sanowa lay down to sleep—that was early in the spring soon after the bluebirds came—our fathers, the bent old gray-heads, kept debating before the Council fire in words like these:

"Yes, look at the son, that thin-nosed, woman-eyed youth with always a smile or a happy look for those he meets. No, the shoulders are not those of a strong man. They never will grow so broad as the father's. And he is not a runner,—no, not even a wrestler. Besides, he stands no taller in his moccasins than a woman. The hands, and even the fingers, are but those of a woman. And yet, shall the youth become a chief of the Osakies?"

"True," others of them gave answer. "True, he is not big, not tall, and not so strong as was the father. True, he is not this, and he is not that; but hush, mark what the people think and say. One day we see that his mother and sister have beaded an oak-leaf upon his moccasins. In the next few days we behold the oak-leaf on the moccasins of other young men. They even plait their hair of a braid same as his. They watch his gesture, they catch the sound of his words; and all that he does, they do, and wherever he goes, they go. Look also at the women, the younger women. Why do they lift their eyes from the sewing when they see him pass? And why do they slacken step in the path from the spring with their vessels of water, and glance from the corner of their eyes at him stepping by?"

Thus back and forth over the Council fire, our fathers talked of the son of Sanowa. But there came an end of it all at last.

One day in the *Nepeni Kisheswa*, the moon that ripens the corn, most of the men and women and even children were in the fields, down in the valley, gathering corn. Suddenly at midday, when the sunshine came down whitest, runners burst through the lodges yelling, "Comanches over the river coming this way! Comanches over the river coming this way!"

Now the story would be long to tell of the alarm spreading among the harvesters; how the braves and the warriors flew to arms, and how as they met the Comanche in the valley, on the banks, and in the water of the river itself, our fathers back yonder among the lodges gathered about the sacred drum, and beat upon it a measure to which the women kept time as they sang the war songs of the nation; how in the evening by the firelight, our fathers put up the scalp-pole, at the top of which they had hung the Comanche scalp-locks newly won that day in the battle; and how as they seated themselves by it, they watched warrior after warrior step slowly out of the dark and stand before them to receive an eagle feather from his gens; and how finally, by the aid of their canes, they pulled themselves to their feet on hearing Sanowa's old warrior, Kewanat, say, as he stuck an eagle feather into the hair of a youth who came up last of all the warriors, "Wakamo, your gens gives you this because you were first at the river and the last to leave off fighting the Comanches."

While the embers of the scalp-dance fire were flickering low, while the people were silently filing off to their lodges, and the warriors on guard were signalling to one another the calls of animals and birds of the night, Wakamo busied himself with persuading the elders to let him go at the head of his father's warriors into the country of the Comanches. There, in the stillness of night, they gave him his father's war bundle, telling him solemnly, as they gave it, to keep it as became an Osakie and a son of Sanowa.

Our men had been in the Comanche country ever since the morning, and as the scouts went spying ahead, they scattered themselves far enough apart to catch a signal one waved to the other. The sun was halfway down the western sky when a scout near the top of a prairie hill far in advance gestured with arm and hand that buffaloes were feeding beyond in the plain below. From scout to scout behind him flew the message to Wakamo, who was coming up with the main body of our men. Back in the same manner flew the gestures of Wakamo, signalling for the scouts to hide on the hill where the farthest scout was, till he and the rest had caught up. Then up the hill went our men, silently and stealthily picking their way. But hardly had half of them reached the place where the scouts lay, when suddenly a rumble, like the grumbling of the Thunderers, rolled over the plain where the buffaloes were browsing. Instantly all who had come crawled to the ridge and peered over. Behold! the buffaloes were making away from the hill on a wild stampede; and as the men straightened their backs and rose from their knees, they caught sight of wolves emerging from hollows and out of patches of reeds. Wakamo yelped. Instantly they sprang to their hind feet, and lo! Comanches stood before them. For as fast as they stood erect, they flung back from their heads and shoulders the wolf-skins with which they had covered themselves to decoy the buffaloes.

At the sight of them slapping their breasts, waving their bows and their arrows in air, and defiantly whooping a challenge to battle, Kewanat touched Wakamo upon the shoulder, and both stepped out in front of and apart from the rest. Each then took from a buckskin knot at the wrist a pinch of *natawinona*, the powdered dust of a sacred herb that grew in the shades and unfrequented retreats of the forests and valleys on the Mississippi. Facing the north-east sky, towards the land of their lodges, they sprinkled the *natawinona* to the wind, and muttered a prayer to Gisha Munetoa and to the spirit of Sanowa. Then Wakamo faced about, and whooped the *Wawaka-hamowina*, the battle yell of his father's warriors. They at once yelled it back, and all pushed downhill on the run; and as they went they strung their bows and whipped out their arrows from the quivers they had fixed under the arm at the side.

On reaching the foot of the hill, they found that they were three or four to one of the Comanches. But so fast and thick and sure whizzed the Comanche arrows that our men were brought to a standing fight at arrow range. The Comanches fought like buffalo bulls, and it looked as if they would drive the Osakies back up the hill.

By and by a lull fell over the fight. The Comanches were falling short of arrows, and so began to run to one of their number who was calling aloud to them; and as fast as they put into his quiver and hand what arrows they had, they whirled into the buffalo trail and ran at the top of their speed.

The Osakies at once pushed forward in pursuit; but no sooner had they started than they stopped, amazed at the sight of the armed Comanche who, standing in their way, pulled his bow back as far as the point of the arrow, and drew a sweeping aim at their whole front as if to fight them alone. And as they stopped, he let fly the arrow, bringing down an Osakie. Instantly he turned and was off as fast as he could go after the other Comanches. Again our men pursued; and, once more, when they pressed the Comanche close, he faced about and pierced another Osakie, bringing, as he shot, all of our men to a stop. The next instant he was off, and another time our men pushed after him. On and on over the plain our men chased after the Comanche, stopping when he faced about and leaping after him when he turned his back. And as they ran, they stuck arrows in the ground at his heels, sent them whirring and hissing past every part of his body, but never did they once graze his skin. And all the while his friends were getting farther away out of the reach of our men.

Why it was the Comanche shot so well and our bowmen were unable to hit him, is not for us to say. Who knows but that a *munetoa*, a divinity, gave him courage to fight so many alone, turned aside our arrows, and guided the course of his? It was a strange fight, wonderfully strange. Feeling somehow that they could not hit him, our men coaxed and cajoled and yelled to one another to fling themselves with all their might into the pursuit with the hope of capturing the Comanche. And, at that, they shoved on all the harder, puffing as they went.

The Comanche's knees got to wabbling and his body to swaying from side to side as he ran. Then he got to drawing and aiming his bow without letting go the arrow. He did this once, twice, three times, and then Wakamo caught sight of the feathered tip of only a single arrow sticking out of the Comanche's quiver.

"Only one arrow he has, my men!" Wakamo yelled aloud as the Comanche shot away the one in the bow. "Don't stop when he shoots, but rush upon him and take him captive alive!"

As the Osakies rushed and closed in upon him, he faced them like a warrior. He drew back the bow with all the strength that he had. But when he aimed, it was up at the sky. And lo! when he let go the arrow, and it flew over the heads of our men, his legs gave way beneath him; and at the very instant that Wakamo was about to lay hands upon him, the Comanche sank to the grass dead.

Panting and all in a sweat, our men crowded in a circle about the Comanche lying there young and tall and sinewy, without even a speck of a wound upon his body. Their eyes rolled with wonder as they looked him over from head to foot. For a while at first the wail of the wind only might have been heard. Presently Wakamo whispered, "A fighter!" "Yes, and like a hawk!" mumbled Kewa-nat. Instantly, "A man!" "A warrior!" and a multitude of other such words fell to buzzing from the lips of the men leaning upon their bows. Suddenly a hush dropped over them all, bringing again the silence. Kewanat knelt at the side of the Comanche, and as he wiped the blade of his knife on the palm of his hand, said:

"My young chief, and my kinsmen, here is a man who was truly a warrior. For you see what he has done. He has kept us from cap-turing him; he has kept us from slaying him with our own hands. More than that, he has enabled his own to escape and flee out of our reach. I shall not tell you that you are good warriors, nor that you are not. But *here* lies a warrior. I shall take out his heart, and show you the heart of a brave man. And after you have seen it, eat of it. You will then be brave, too."

Kewanat then cut open the flesh over the left of the breast along the hollow between two ribs. Spreading apart the ribs, he reached in his hand, and when he withdrew it, the eyes of the men were filled all the more with wonder; for between finger and thumb hung a heart no bigger perhaps than a sandhill plum. It was small, too small it seemed, for the heart of a man. It was like gristle and as tough as gristle.

"No," muttered Kewanat, shaking his head as he held the heart out at arm's length. "No, we will not eat of it. It is too small to go all round. But that is not all. The Comanche fought us like a warrior when he was alive. Let him then in death keep his heart. It tells us, besides, that the heart of a brave man is small, small like this."

After Kewanat had replaced the heart within the breast, he bent over, and fingered the Comanche's scalp-lock.

"Oh, my young chief," he said, looking up at Wakamo who stood thoughtfully beside him, "that hanging in your lodge would be worthier by far than any your father ever took from Sioux, Osage, or Cheyenne. But your father never would have scalped a warrior like this. We are leaving him his heart, shall we also leave him the scalp?"

Wakamo nodded and slowly replied, "Yes. Let him keep it. There will be wailing enough in a lodge of the Comanches, and it may gladden the hearts of those in that lodge to know how bravely he fell."

Our men then dropped in behind Wakamo and Kewanat, glancing over their shoulders as they filed away for a last look at the Comanche. The bodies of their dead they took to the top of the hill from which they had first seen the Comanches. There they buried them, piling over them a mound of earth and stones.

While our men were resting and spying for a stream where they might camp, the sun was nearing the banks of the Great River in the west, the river that plunges and roars and foams between this world and the next. And as they were beholding the glow that lit up the western sky, their eyes fell upon three men leaving the spot where the Comanche had died. Their course was westward. One of them went ahead; the other two followed behind, carrying a burden upon their shoulders.

Our men came home before the first fall of snow. They said little about Comanche scalp-locks at the dance and the feast that welcomed them home. But by the fire of the lodge, the kin seated closely about and listening with open ear and expectant look, each told of a heart that makes a brave man, a little heart like that of the young Comanche. As our fathers one after the other heard the story, they rose and told it to others. When they had all heard it, they went to the Council lodge. And there they joyfully smoked their long redstone pipe; joyfully, because the young Wakamo had seen with his own eyes what made a brave man, and because they felt that the son would now surely grow to be the chief that his father was.

Francis La Flesche

Francis La Flesche was born on December 25, 1857, on the Omaha Reservation in what is now Nebraska. His father, Estamaza (Iron Eye), was of part French descent and was the leader of a progressive faction favoring adoption of Anglo ways. His Omaha mother, Elizabeth Esau, was Iron Eye's second wife. He was the stepbrother of Susette La Flesche (Bright Eyes) and Dr. Susan La Flesche-Picotte, one of the first female Indian physicians.

Francis La Flesche received his education at the Presbyterian mission school at Bellevue, Nebraska. He later recorded his experiences there in *The Middle Five* (Boston: Small, Mayard and Co., 1900; reprint, Lincoln: University of Nebraska Press, 1978). In his early twenties he accompanied Chief Standing Bear (together with Susette) on his celebrated tour of the East in 1879 and 1880. The following year he was appointed as a copyist in the Office of Indian Affairs, where he remained until 1910. While in that service he also studied law at National University, receiving an L.L.B. degree in 1892 and an L.L.M. a year later. In 1910 he transferred to the Bureau of American Ethnology, for which he worked until his retirement in 1929. Francis La Flesche was a member of the American Anthropological Society and was president of the Anthropological Society of Washington in 1922–23. In recognition of his scholarly achievements in the field of anthropology, he was awarded an honorary doctorate in 1926 by the University of Nebraska.

In the years between 1881 and 1923 La Flesche was Alice Fletcher's primary informant on the Omaha. This cooperation finally resulted in the classic study *The Omaha Tribe* (*Twenty-seventh Annual Report of the Bureau of American Ethnology, 1911*, pp. 17–654). La Flesche also conducted extensive research on the Osage, and part of his findings, known collectively as *The Osage Tribe*, was published in the Bureau's thirty-sixth, thirty-ninth, forty-third, and forty-fifth annual reports between 1914 and 1928, as well as the *Dictionary of the Osage Language* (Bureau of American Ethnology, Bulletin 109, 1932). He also left behind a nearly completed dictionary of the Omaha language and volumes of unpublished manuscripts deposited in the Smithsonian Institution. Among the numerous shorter writings he published between 1885 and 1926 there were apparently only two pieces that could be considered short stories, one of them based on legend. Finally, he joined composer Charles Wakefield Cadman in writing an American Indian grand opera in three acts titled "Da-Oma, the Land of the Misty Waters." It was completed in 1912 but never produced. La Flesche died on September 5, 1932, in Nebraska.

REFERENCES

Alexander, H. B. "Francis La Flesche." *American Anthropologist* 35 (April–June 1933): 328–331.
Green, Norma Kidd. *Iron Eye's Family: The Children of Joseph La Flesche.* Lincoln, Nebr.: Johnson Publishing Company, 1969.
Liberty, Margot. "Francis La Flesche: The Osage Odyssey, 1857–1932." In Margot Liberty, ed., *American Indian Intellectuals*, 44–59. Proceedings of the American Ethnological Society, 1976. St. Paul: West Publishing Company, 1978.

STORIES BY FRANCIS LA FLESCHE

"The Story of a Vision." *Southern Workman*, February 1901, 106–109.
"One Touch of Nature." *Southern Workman*, August 1913, 427–428.

The Story of a Vision

FRANCIS LA FLESCHE

Each of us, as we gathered at the lodge of our story teller at dusk, picked up an armful of wood and entered. The old man who was sitting alone, his wife having gone on a visit, welcomed us with a pleasant word as we threw the wood down by the fire-place and busied ourselves rekindling the fire.

Ja-bae-ka and Ne-ne-ba, having nothing to do at this moment, fell to scuffling. "You will be fighting if you keep on," warned the old man.

"Stop your fooling and come and sit down," scolded Wa-du-pa; "you're not in your own house."

The flames livened up cheerily and cast a ruddy glow about us, when Wa-du-pa said, "Grandfather, the last time we were here you told us the myth of the eagle and the wren; we liked it, but now we want a true story, something that really happened, something you saw yourself."

"How thirsty I am!" said the old man irrelevantly, "I wonder what makes me so dry."

"Quick!" said Wa-du-pa, motioning to Ja-bae-ka, "Get some water!"

The lad peered into one kettle, squinted into another and then said, "There isn't any."

"Then go, get some!" arose a number of voices.

"Why don't some of you go?" Ja-bae-ka retorted, picking up one of the kettles.

"Take both!" some one shouted.

Ja-bae-ka approached the door grumbling. As he grasped the heavy skin portier to make his way out, he turned and said, "Don't begin until I come back."

We soon heard his heavy breathing in the long entrance way. "It's moonlight, just like day!" he exclaimed, as he set the kettles down and thrust his cold hands into the flames with a twisting motion. "The boys and girls are having lots of fun sliding on the ice."

"Let them slide, we don't care!" ejaculated Wa-du-pa as he dipped a cup into the water and handed it to the old man, who put it to his lips and made a gulping sound as he drank, the lump in his throat leaping up and down at each swallow. At the last draught he expelled his pent-up breath with something like a groan, set the cup down, wiped his lips with the back of his hand, and asked, "A real true story—something that I saw myself; that's what you want, is it?"

"Yes, grandfather," we sang out in chorus, "a story that has you in it!"

His face brightened with a smile and he broke into a gentle laugh, nodding his head to its rhythm.

After a few moments' musing, and when we boys had settled down, the old man began:

Many, many winters ago, long before any of you were born, our people went on a winter hunt, away out among the sand hills where even now we sometimes go. There was a misunderstanding between the leaders, so that just as we reached the hunting grounds the tribe separated into two parties, each going in a different direction.

The weather was pleasant enough while on the journey, but a few days after the departure of our friends a heavy storm came upon us. For days and nights the wind howled and roared, threatening to carry away our tents, and the snow fell thick and fast, so that we could not see an arm's length; it was waist deep and yet it kept falling. No hunting could be done; food grew scarcer and scarcer and the older people became alarmed.

One afternoon as my father, mother and I were sitting in our tent eating from our last kettle of corn, there came a lull and we heard with startling distinctness a man singing a song of augury. We paused to listen, but the wind swept down again and drowned the voice.

"A holy man seeking for a sign," said my father. "Son, go and hear if he will give us words of courage."

My father was lame and could not go himself, so I waded through the heavy drifts and with much difficulty reached the man's tent, where many were already gathered to hear the predictions. I held my breath in awe as I heard the holy man say:

"For a moment the wind ceased to blow, the clouds parted, and in the rift I saw standing, in mid air against the blue sky, the spirit of the man who was murdered last summer. His head was bowed in grief and although he spoke not, I know from the vision that the anger of the storm gods was moved against us for not punishing the murderer. Silently the spirit lifted an arm and pointed beyond the hills. Then I found that I too was in mid air. I looked over the hilltops and beheld a forest, where shadowy forms like those of large animals moved among the trees. I turned once more to the spirit, but the clouds had come together again.

"Before dawn to-morrow the storm will pass away, then let the runners go to the forest that I saw and tell us whether or not there is truth in the words that I have spoken."

As predicted, the wind ceased to blow and the snow to fall. Runners were hastily sent to the forest and the sun was hardly risen when one of them returned with the good news that the shadowy forms the holy man had seen were truly those of buffalo.

The effect of the news upon the camp was like magic, faces brightened, the gloomy forebodings that clouded the minds of the older people fled as did the storm, and laughter and pleasantries enlivened the place. The hunters and boys were soon plodding through the snow toward the forest and before dark everyone returned heavily laden, tired and hungry, but none the less happy. The fires burned brightly that night and men told stories until it was nearly morning.

The forest of the vision was a bag of game; every few days the hunters went there and returned with buffalo, elk, or deer, so that even the poorest man had plenty for his wife and children to eat.

All this time nothing had been heard from the party that separated from us before the storm. One night when I came home from a rabbit hunt, I found my mother and father packing up pemican and jerked meat as though for a journey. I looked inquiringly at the pack as I ate my supper; bye and bye my mother told me that a man had just come from the other camp with the news that the people had exhausted their supplies and, as they could find no game, they were suffering for want of food. My sister and her husband were in that camp, and I was told to carry the pack to them.

My father had arranged with a young man bound on a similar errand to call for me early in the morning, so I went to bed as soon as I had finished eating, to get as much sleep and rest as possible. It was well that I did, for long before dawn creaking footsteps approached our tent and the man called out, "Are you ready?" I quickly slipped on my leggings and moccasins, put on my robe, slung the pack over my shoulders and we started.

To avoid the drifts we followed the ridges, but even there the snow lay deep and we were continually breaking through the hard crust. My friend turned every mishap into a joke and broke the monotony of our travel with humorous tales and incidents. Late at night we camped in the bend of a small, wooded stream. We gathered a big pile of dry branches, kindled a roaring fire and roasted some of the jerked meat. When supper was over we dried our moccasins, then piling more wood on the fire we wrapped ourselves up in our robes and went to sleep.

I do not know how long we might have slept had we not been wakened by the howling of hundreds of wolves not far away from us. "They're singing to the morning star!" said my friend. "It is near day, so we must be up and going."

We ate a little of the pemican, helped each other to load, and again we started. Before night we were overtaken by other men and boys who were also going to the relief of their friends in the other camp, where we arrived just in time to save many of the people from starving.

How curious it was that the predictions of the holy man should come true—the stopping of the storm before morning, the forest, and the shadowy forms of animals. Stranger still was the death of the murderer. This took place, we were told by the people we had rescued, on the very night of the augury in our camp. They said, as the man was sitting in his tent that night, the wind suddenly blew the door flap violently aside, an expression of terror come over his face, he fell backward, and he was dead.

In the old days, many strange things came to pass in the life of our people, but now we are getting to be different.

Wa-du-pa thanked the story teller, and we were about to go when Ne-ne-ba, pointing to Ja-bae-ka, whispered, "He's gone to sleep! Let's scare him."

The old man fell into the spirit of the fun, so we all tip-toed to the back part of the lodge where it was dark and watched, as the flames died down to a blue flickering. We could see the boy's head drop lower and lower until his nose nearly touched his knee. Just then a log on the fire suddenly tumbled from its place, broke in two, sent up a shower of crackling sparks and Ja-bae-ka awoke with a start. He threw up his head, looked all around and thinking he was left alone in the darkened lodge, took fright and rushed to the door with a cry of terror. We ran out of our hiding places with shouts of laughter and overtook Ja-bae-ka outside the door, where we teased him about going to sleep and being afraid in the dark.

Suddenly he turned upon Ne-ne-ba and said, "You did that, you rascal! I'll pay you back sometime."

Gertrude Bonnin

✳

Gertrude Simmons Bonnin was born on February 22, 1876, on the Yankton Sioux Agency in South Dakota. She was raised by her full-blood mother, Ellen Simmons; her father appears to have been an Anglo-American. She later took up the pen name Zitkala-Sa, or Red Bird.

Bonnin attended White's Indiana Manual Labor Institute in Wabash, a Quaker missionary school for Indians, and completed her studies in 1897 at Earlham College in Richmond, Indiana. She then taught at the Carlisle Indian School for two years prior to enrolling at the Boston Conservatory of Music. In 1900 she accompanied the Carlisle Indian Band as a violin soloist on a trip to the Paris Exposition.

Bonnin began her literary career at the turn of the century, publishing three autobiographical sketches in the *Atlantic Monthly* and three short stories in *Harper's Monthly* and *Everybody's Magazine* between 1900 and 1902. In 1901 she published a collection of Sioux tales titled *Old Indian Legends* (Boston: Ginn & Co.; reprint, Lincoln: University of Nebraska Press, 1985). At this time she also established a reputation as a public speaker, a talent she had already developed during her sojourn at Earlham College.

In 1901 Bonnin met Carlos Montezuma, the noted Yavapai physician and journalist. Their plans to marry never materialized, however, and in 1902 she took up the position of issue clerk at the Standing Rock Reservation, where she met and married Raymond Bonnin that same year. With her husband she moved to the Uintah Reservation in Utah, where she was to remain for the next fourteen years.

Around 1913 Gertrude Bonnin began to correspond with the Society of American Indians, and she joined its advisory board in

1914. A year later she started a community-center project at Uintah that was much publicized by the SAI. In 1916 she was elected as the society's secretary and thereupon moved to Washington, D.C. In 1918 and 1919 she also edited the SAI's journal, the *American Indian Magazine*. After the SAI disbanded, she established the National Council of American Indians, remaining president and editor of its *Indian Newsletter* until her death. Her political activities brought her into contact with the General Federation of Women's Clubs, and she helped to form its Indian Welfare Committee, which, along with the Indian Rights Association, sponsored an investigation of illegal appropriations of Oklahoma Indian lands (see Gertrude Bonnin, Charles H. Fabens, and Mathew K. Sniffen, *Oklahoma's Poor Rich Indians: An Orgy of Graft and Exploitation of the Five Civilized Tribes—Legalized Robbery* [Philadelphia: Office of the Indian Rights Association, 1924]).

During the 1920s Bonnin strongly supported John Collier, who introduced her to people like Mabel Dodge and Mary Austin. By 1932 their relation had become strained, however, and she ultimately opposed the acceptance of the Indian Reorganization Act at the Yankton Agency.

In contrast to her political fervor, Bonnin's literary productivity decreased markedly during the latter part of her life. In 1921 she published *American Indian Stories* (Washington, D.C.: Hayworth Press; reprint, Lincoln: University of Nebraska Press, 1985), which was basically a reprint of her previous sketches and short stories. Somewhat earlier, in 1913, she had joined William E. Hanson in composing an Indian opera titled *Sun Dance*. It was selected in 1937 as the American opera of the year by the New York Light Opera Guild. Gertrude Bonnin died on January 26, 1938, in Washington, D.C.

REFERENCES

Fisher, Dexter. "Zitkala-Sa: The Evolution of a Writer." *American Indian Quarterly* 5 (Fall 1979): 229–238.

———. "The Transformation of Tradition: A Study of Zitkala-Sa and

Mourning Dove, Two Transitional American Indian Writers." In Andrew Wiget, ed., *Critical Essays on Native American Literature*, 202–211. Boston: G. K. Hall & Company, 1985.

Gridley, Marion. *American Indian Women*. New York: Hawthorne Books, 1974.

James, Edward T., ed. *Notable American Women, 1607–1950*. Cambridge, Mass.: Harvard University Press, 1971.

STORIES BY GERTRUDE BONNIN

"The Soft-Hearted Sioux." *Harper's Monthly*, October 1901, 505–508.

"A Warrior's Daughter." *Everybody's Magazine*, April 6, 1902, 346–352.

"The Trial Path." *Harper's Monthly*, March 1901, 741–744.

"Shooting of the Red Eagle." *Indian Reader*, August 1904, 1.

The Soft-Hearted Sioux

ZITKALA-SA [GERTRUDE BONNIN]

I

Beside the open fire I sat within our tepee. With my red blanket wrapped tightly about my crossed legs, I was thinking of the coming season, my sixteenth winter. On either side of the wigwam were my parents. My father was whistling a tune between his teeth while polishing with his bare hand a red stone pipe he had recently carved. Almost in front of me, beyond the centre fire, my old grandmother sat near the entranceway.

She turned her face toward her right and addressed most of her words to my mother. Now and then she spoke to me, but never did she allow her eyes to rest upon her daughter's husband, my father. It was only upon rare occasions that my grandmother said anything to him. Thus his ears were open and ready to catch the smallest wish she might express. Sometimes when my grandmother had been saying things which pleased him, my father used to comment upon them. At other times, when he could not approve of what was spoken, he used to work or smoke silently.

On this night my old grandmother began her talk about me. Filling the bowl of her red stone pipe with dry willow bark, she looked across at me.

"My grandchild, you are tall and are no longer a little boy." Narrowing her old eyes, she asked, "My grandchild, when are you going to bring here a handsome young woman?" I stared into the fire rather than meet her gaze. Waiting for my answer, she stooped forward and through the long stem drew a flame into the red stone pipe.

I smiled while my eyes were still fixed upon the bright fire, but I said nothing in reply. Turning to my mother, she offered her the

78

pipe. I glanced at my grandmother. The loose buckskin sleeve fell off at her elbow and showed a wrist covered with silver bracelets. Holding up the fingers of her left hand, she named off the desirable young women of our village.

"Which one, my grandchild, which one?" she questioned.

"Hoh!" I said, pulling at my blanket in confusion. "Not yet!" Here my mother passed the pipe over the fire to my father. Then she too began speaking of what I should do.

"My son, be always active. Do not dislike a long hunt. Learn to provide much buffalo meat and many buckskins before you bring home a wife." Presently my father gave the pipe to my grandmother, and he took his turn in the exhortations.

"Ho, my son, I have been counting in my heart the bravest warriors of our people. There is not one of them who won his title in his sixteenth winter. My son, it is a great thing for some brave of sixteen winters to do."

Not a word had I to give in answer. I knew well the fame of my warrior father. He had earned the right of speaking such words, though even he himself was a brave only at my age. Refusing to smoke my grandmother's pipe because my heart was too much stirred by their words, and sorely troubled with a fear lest I should disappoint them, I arose to go. Drawing my blanket over my shoulders, I said, as I stepped toward the entranceway: "I go to hobble my pony. It is now late in the night."

II

Nine winters' snows had buried deep that night when my old grandmother, together with my father and mother, designed my future with the glow of a camp fire upon it.

Yet I did not grow up the warrior, huntsman, and husband I was to have been. At the mission school I learned it was wrong to kill. Nine winters I hunted for the soft heart of Christ, and prayed for the huntsmen who chased the buffalo on the plains.

In the autumn of the tenth year I was sent back to my tribe to preach Christianity to them. With the white man's Bible in my hand, and the white man's tender heart in my breast, I returned to my own people.

Wearing a foreigner's dress, I walked, a stranger, into my father's village.

Asking my way, for I had not forgotten my native tongue, an old man led me toward the tepee where my father lay. From my old companion I learned that my father had been sick many moons. As we drew near the tepee, I heard the chanting of a medicine-man within it. At once I wished to enter in and drive from my home the sorcerer of the plains, but the old warrior checked me. "Ho, wait outside until the medicine-man leaves your father," he said. While talking he scanned me from head to feet. Then he retraced his steps toward the heart of the camping-ground.

My father's dwelling was on the outer limits of the round-faced village. With every heart-throb I grew more impatient to enter the wigwam.

While I turned the leaves of my Bible with nervous fingers, the medicine-man came forth from the dwelling and walked hurriedly away. His head and face were closely covered with the loose robe which draped his entire figure.

He was tall and large. His long strides I have never forgot. They seemed to me then as the uncanny gait of eternal death. Quickly pocketing my Bible, I went into the tepee.

Upon a mat lay my father, with furrowed face and gray hair. His eyes and cheeks were sunken far into his head. His sallow skin lay thin upon his pinched nose and high cheek-bones. Stooping over him, I took his fevered hand. "How, Ate?" I greeted him. A light flashed from his listless eyes and his dried lips parted. "My son!" he murmured, in a feeble voice. Then again the wave of joy and rec- ognition receded. He closed his eyes, and his hand dropped from my open palm to the ground.

Looking about, I saw an old woman sitting with bowed head. Shaking hands with her, I recognized my mother. I sat down be- tween my father and mother as I used to do, but I did not feel at home. The place where my old grandmother used to sit was now unoccupied. With my mother I bowed my head. Alike our throats were choked and tears were streaming from our eyes; but far apart in spirit our ideas and faiths separated us. My grief was for the soul unsaved; and I thought my mother wept to see a brave man's body broken by sickness.

Useless was my attempt to change the faith in the medicine-man to that abstract power named God. Then one day I became righteously mad with anger that the medicine-man should thus ensnare my father's soul. And when he came to chant his sacred songs I pointed toward the door and bade him go! The man's eyes glared upon me for an instant. Slowly gathering his robe about him, he turned his back upon the sick man and stepped out of our wigwam. "Hā, hā, hā! my son, I cannot live without the medicine-man!" I heard my father cry when the sacred man was gone.

III

On a bright day, when the winged seeds of the prairie-grass were flying hither and thither, I walked solemnly toward the centre of the camping-ground. My heart beat hard and irregularly at my side. Tighter I grasped the sacred book I carried under my arm. Now was the beginning of life's work.

Though I knew it would be hard, I did not once feel that failure was to be my reward. As I stepped unevenly on the rolling ground, I thought of the warriors soon to wash off their war-paints and follow me.

At length I reached the place where the people had assembled to hear me preach. In a large circle men and women sat upon the dry red grass. Within the ring I stood, with the white man's Bible in my hand. I tried to tell them of the soft heart of Christ.

In silence the vast circle of bareheaded warriors sat under an afternoon sun. At last, wiping the wet from my brow, I took my place in the ring. The hush of the assembly filled me with great hope.

I was turning my thoughts upward to the sky in gratitude, when a stir called me to earth again.

A tall, strong man arose. His loose robe hung in folds over his right shoulder. A pair of snapping black eyes fastened themselves like the poisonous fangs of a serpent upon me. He was the medicine-man. A tremor played about my heart and a chill cooled the fire in my veins.

Scornfully he pointed a long forefinger in my direction and asked, "What loyal son is he who, returning to his father's people, wears a foreigner's dress?" He paused a moment, and then continued: "The dress of that foreigner of whom a story says he bound a native of our land, and heaping dry sticks around him, kindled a fire at his feet!" Waving his hand toward me, he exclaimed, "Here is the traitor to his people!"

I was helpless. Before the eyes of the crowd the cunning magician turned my honest heart into a vile nest of treachery. Alas! the people frowned as they looked upon me.

"Listen!" he went on. "Which one of you who have eyed the young man can see through his bosom and warn the people of the nest of young snakes hatching there? Whose ear was so acute that he caught the hissing of snakes whenever the young man opened his mouth? This one has not only proven false to you, but even to the Great Spirit who made him. He is a fool! Why do you sit here giving ear to a foolish man who could not defend his people because he fears to kill, who could not bring venison to renew the life of his sick father? With his prayers, let him drive away the enemy! With his soft heart, let him keep off starvation! We shall go elsewhere to dwell upon an untainted ground."

With this he disbanded the people. When the sun lowered in the west and the winds were quiet, the village of cone-shaped tepees was gone. The medicine-man had won the hearts of the people.

Only my father's dwelling was left to mark the fighting-ground.

IV

From a long night at my father's bedside I came out to look upon the morning. The yellow sun hung equally between the snow-covered land and the cloudless blue sky. The light of the new day was cold. The strong breath of winter crusted the snow and fitted crystal shells over the rivers and lakes. As I stood in front of the tepee, thinking of the vast prairies which separated us from our tribe, and wondering if the high sky likewise separated the soft-hearted Son of God from us, the icy blast from the north blew through my hair and skull. My neglected hair had grown long and fell upon my neck.

My father had not risen from his bed since the day the medicine-man led the people away. Though I read from the Bible and prayed beside him upon my knees, my father would not listen. Yet I believed my prayers were not unheeded in heaven.

"Hā, hā, hā! my son," my father groaned upon the first snowfall. "My son, our food is gone. There is no one to bring me meat! My son, your soft heart has unfitted you for everything!" Then covering his face with the buffalo-robe, he said no more. Now while I stood out in that cold winter morning, I was starving. For two days I had not seen any food. But my own cold and hunger did not harass my soul as did the whining cry of the sick old man.

Stepping again into the tepee, I untied my snow-shoes, which were fastened to the tent-poles.

My poor mother, watching by the sick one, and faithfully heaping wood upon the centre fire, spoke to me:

"My son, do not fail again to bring your father meat, or he will starve to death."

"How, Ina," I answered, sorrowfully. From the tepee I started forth again to hunt food for my aged parents. All day I tracked the white level lands in vain. Nowhere, nowhere were there any other footprints but my own! In the evening of this third fast-day I came back without meat. Only a bundle of sticks for the fire I brought on my back. Dropping the wood outside, I lifted the door-flap and set one foot within the tepee.

There I grew dizzy and numb. My eyes swam in tears. Before me lay my old gray-haired father sobbing like a child. In his horny hands he clutched the buffalo-robe, and with his teeth he was gnawing off the edges. Chewing the dry stiff hair and buffalo-skin, my father's eyes sought my hands. Upon seeing them empty, he cried out:

"My son, your soft heart will let me starve before you bring me meat! Two hills eastward stand a herd of cattle. Yet you will see me die before you bring me food!"

Leaving my mother lying with covered head upon her mat, I rushed out into the night.

With a strange warmth in my heart and swiftness in my feet, I climbed over the first hill, and soon the second one. The moonlight upon the white country showed me a clear path to the white man's cattle. With my hand upon the knife in my belt, I leaned heavily against the fence while counting the herd.

Twenty in all I numbered. From among them I chose the best-fattened creature. Leaping over the fence, I plunged my knife into it.

My long knife was sharp, and my hands, no more fearful and slow, slashed off choice chunks of warm flesh. Bending under the meat I had taken for my starving father, I hurried across the prairie.

Toward home I fairly ran with the life-giving food I carried upon my back. Hardly had I climbed the second hill when I heard sounds coming after me. Faster and faster I ran with my load for my father, but the sounds were gaining upon me. I heard the clicking of snow-shoes and the squeaking of the leather straps at my heels; yet I did not turn to see what pursued me, for I was intent upon reaching my father. Suddenly like thunder an angry voice shouted curses and threats into my ear! A rough hand wrenched my shoulder and took the meat from me! I stopped struggling to run. A deafening whir filled my head. The moon and stars began to move. Now the white prairie was sky, and the stars lay under my feet. Now again they were turning. At last the starry blue rose up into place. The noise in my ears was still. A great quiet filled the air. In my hand I found my long knife dripping with blood. At my feet a man's figure lay prone in blood-red snow. The horrible scene about me seemed a trick of my senses, for I could not understand it was real. Looking long upon the blood-stained snow, the load of meat for my starving father reached my recognition at last. Quickly I tossed it over my shoulder and started again homeward.

Tired and haunted I reached the door of the wigwam. Carrying the food before me, I entered with it into the tepee.

"Father, here is food!" I cried, as I dropped the meat near my mother. No answer came. Turning about, I beheld my gray-haired father dead! I saw by the unsteady firelight an old gray-haired skeleton lying rigid and stiff.

Out into the open I started, but the snow at my feet became bloody.

V

On the day after my father's death, having led my mother to the camp of the medicine-man, I gave myself up to those who were searching for the murderer of the paleface.

They bound me hand and foot. Here in this cell I was placed four days ago.

The shrieking winter winds have followed me hither. Rattling the bars, they howl unceasingly: "Your soft heart! your soft heart will see me die before you bring me food!" Hark! something is clanking the chain on the door. It is being opened. From the dark night without a black figure crosses the threshold. . . . It is the guard. He comes to warn me of my fate. He tells me that tomorrow I must die. In his stern face I laugh aloud. I do not fear death.

Yet I wonder who shall come to welcome me in the realm of strange sight. Will the loving Jesus grant me pardon and give my soul a soothing sleep? or will my warrior father greet me and receive me as his son? Will my spirit fly upward to a happy heaven? or shall I sink into the bottomless pit, an outcast from a God of infinite love?

Soon, soon I shall know, for now I see the east is growing red. My heart is strong. My face is calm. My eyes are dry and eager for new scenes. My hands hang quietly at my side. Serene and brave, my soul awaits the men to perch me on the gallows for another flight. I go.

A Warrior's Daughter

ZITKALA-SA [GERTRUDE BONNIN]

In the afternoon shadow of a large teepee, with red-painted smoke lapels, sat a warrior father with crossed shins. His head was so poised that his eye swept easily the vast level land to the eastern horizon line.

He was the chieftain's bravest warrior. He had won by heroic deeds the privilege of staking his wigwam within the great circle of teepees.

He was also one of the most generous gift givers to the toothless old people. For this he was entitled to the red-painted smoke lapels on his cone-shaped dwelling. He was proud of his honors. He never wearied of rehearsing nightly his own brave deeds. Though by wigwam fires he prated much of his high rank and widespread fame, his great joy was a wee black-eyed daughter of eight sturdy winters. Thus as he sat upon the soft grass, with his wife at his side, bent over her bead work, he was singing a dance song, and beat lightly the rhythm with his slender hands.

His shrewd eyes softened with pleasure as he watched the easy movements of the small body dancing on the green before him.

Tusee is taking her first dancing lesson. Her tightly braided hair curves over both brown ears like a pair of crooked little horns which glisten in the summer sun.

With her snugly moccasined feet close together, and a wee hand at her belt to stay the long string of beads which hang from her bare neck, she bends her knees gently to the rhythm of her father's voice.

Now she ventures upon the earnest movement, slightly upward and sidewise, in a circle. At length the song drops into a closing cadence, and the little woman, clad in beaded deerskin, sits down beside the elder one. Like her mother, she sits upon her feet. In

86

a brief moment the warrior repeats the last refrain. Again Tusee springs to her feet and dances to the swing of the few final measures.

Just as the dance was finished, an elderly man, with short, thick hair loose about his square shoulders, rode into their presence from the rear, and leaped lightly from his pony's back. Dropping the rawhide rein to the ground, he tossed himself lazily on the grass. "Hunhe, you have returned soon," said the warrior, while extending a hand to his little daughter.

Quickly the child ran to her father's side and cuddled close to him, while he tenderly placed a strong arm about her. Both father and child, eyeing the figure on the grass, waited to hear the man's report.

"It is true," began the man, with a stranger's accent. "This is the night of the dance."

"Hunha!" muttered the warrior with some surprise.

Propping himself upon his elbows, the man raised his face. His features were of the southern type. From an enemy's camp he was taken captive long years ago by Tusee's father. But the unusual qualities of the slave had won the Sioux warrior's heart, and for the last three winters the man had had his freedom. He was made a real man again. His hair was allowed to grow. However, he himself had chosen to stay in the warrior's family.

"Hunha!" again ejaculated the warrior father. Then turning to his little daughter, he asked, "Tusee, do you hear that?"

"Yes, father, and I am going to dance to-night!"

With these words she bounded out of his arm and frolicked about in glee. Hereupon the proud mother's voice rang out in a chiding laugh.

"My child, in honor of your first dance your father must give a generous gift. His ponies are wild, and roam beyond the great hill. Pray, what has he fit to offer?" she questioned, the pair of puzzled eyes fixed upon her.

"A pony from the herd, mother, a fleet-footed pony from the herd!" Tusee shouted with sudden inspiration.

Pointing a small forefinger toward the man lying on the grass, she cried, "Uncle, you will go after the pony to-morrow!" And pleased with her solution of the problem, she skipped wildly about. Her childish faith in her elders was not conditioned by a knowledge of human limitations, but thought all things possible to grown-ups.

"Hähob!" exclaimed the mother, with a rising inflection, implying by the expletive that her child's buoyant spirit be not weighted with a denial.

Quickly to the hard request the man replied, "How! I go if Tusee tells me so!"

This delighted the little one, whose black eyes brimmed over with light. Standing in front of the strong man, she clapped her small, brown hands with joy.

"That makes me glad! My heart is good! Go, uncle, and bring a handsome pony!" she cried. In an instant she would have frisked away, but an impulse held her tilting where she stood. In the man's own tongue, for he had taught her many words and phrases, she exploded, "Thank you, good uncle, thank you!" then tore away from sheer excess of glee.

The proud warrior father, smiling and narrowing his eyes, muttered approval, "Howo! Hechetu!"

Like her mother, Tusee has finely pencilled eyebrows and slightly extended nostrils; but in her sturdiness of form she resembles her father.

A loyal daughter, she sits within her teepee making beaded deerskins for her father, while he longs to stave off her every suitor as all unworthy of his old heart's pride. But Tusee is not alone in her dwelling. Near the entrance-way a young brave is half reclining on a mat. In silence he watches the petals of a wild rose growing on the soft buckskin. Quickly the young woman slips the beads on the silvery sinew thread, and works them into the pretty flower design. Finally, in a low, deep voice, the young man begins:

"The sun is far past the zenith. It is now only a man's height above the western edge of land. I hurried hither to tell you to-morrow I join the war party."

He pauses for reply, but the maid's head drops lower over her deerskin, and her lips are more firmly drawn together. He continues:

"Last night in the moonlight I met your warrior father. He seemed to know I had just stepped forth from your teepee. I fear he did not like it, for though I greeted him, he was silent. I halted in his pathway. With what boldness I dared, while my heart was beating hard and fast, I asked him for his only daughter.

"Drawing himself erect to his tallest height, and gathering his loose robe more closely about his proud figure, he flashed a pair of piercing eyes upon me.

" 'Young man,' said he, with a cold, slow voice that chilled me to the marrow of my bones, 'hear me. Naught but an enemy's scalp-lock, plucked fresh with your own hand, will buy Tusee for your wife.' Then he turned on his heel and stalked away."

Tusee thrusts her work aside. With earnest eyes she scans her lover's face.

"My father's heart is really kind. He would know if you are brave and true," murmured the daughter, who wished no ill-will between her two loved ones.

Then rising to go, the youth holds out a right hand. "Grasp my hand once firmly before I go, Hoye. Pray tell me, will you wait and watch for my return?"

Tusee only nods assent, for mere words are vain.

At early dawn the round camp-ground awakes into song. Men and women sing of bravery and of triumph. They inspire the swelling breasts of the painted warriors mounted on prancing ponies bedecked with the green branches of trees.

Riding slowly around the great ring of cone-shaped teepees, here and there, a loud-singing warrior swears to avenge a former wrong, and thrusts a bare brown arm against the purple east, calling the Great Spirit to hear his vow. All having made the circuit, the singing war party gallops away southward.

Astride their ponies laden with food and deerskins, brave elderly women follow after their warriors. Among the foremost rides a young woman in elaborately beaded buckskin dress. Proudly mounted, she curbs with the single rawhide loop a wild-eyed pony.

It is Tusee on her father's warhorse. Thus the war party of Indian men and their faithful women vanish beyond the southern skyline.

A day's journey brings them very near the enemy's borderland. Nightfall finds a pair of twin teepees nestled in a deep ravine. Within one lounge the painted warriors, smoking their pipes and telling weird stories by the firelight, while in the other watchful women crouch uneasily about their centre fire.

By the first gray light in the east the teepees are banished. They are gone. The warriors are in the enemy's camp, breaking dreams with their tomahawks. The women are hid away in secret places in the long thicketed ravine.

The day is far spent, the red sun is low over the west.

At length straggling warriors return, one by one, to the deep hollow. In the twilight they number their men. Three are missing. Of these absent ones two are dead; but the third one, a young man, is a captive to the foe.

"He-he!" lament the warriors, taking food in haste.

In silence each woman, with long strides, hurries to and fro, tying large bundles on her pony's back. Under cover of night the war party must hasten homeward. Motionless, with bowed head, sits a woman in her hiding-place. She grieves for her lover.

In bitterness of spirit she hears the warriors' murmuring words. With set teeth she plans to cheat the hated enemy of their captive. In the meanwhile low signals are given, and the war party, unaware of Tusee's absence, steal quietly away. The soft thud of pony-hoofs grows fainter and fainter. The gradual hush of the empty ravine whirrs noisily in the ear of the young woman. Alert for any sound of footfalls nigh, she holds her breath to listen. Her right hand rests on a long knife in her belt. Ah, yes, she knows where her pony is hid, but not yet has she need of him. Satisfied that no danger is nigh, she prowls forth from her place of hiding. With a panther's tread and pace she climbs the high ridge beyond the low ravine. From thence she spies the enemy's camp-fires.

Rooted to the barren bluff the slender woman's figure stands on the pinnacle of night, outlined against a starry sky. The cool night breeze wafts to her burning ear snatches of song and drum. With desperate hate she bites her teeth.

Tusee beckons the stars to witness. With impassioned voice and uplifted face she pleads:

"Great Spirit, speed me to my lover's rescue! Give me swift cunning for a weapon this night! All-powerful Spirit, grant me my warrior-father's heart, strong to slay a foe and mighty to save a friend!"

In the midst of the enemy's camp-ground, underneath a temporary dance-house, are men and women in gala-day dress. It is late in the night, but the merry warriors bend and bow their nude, painted bodies before a bright centre fire. To the lusty men's voices and the rhythmic throbbing drum, they leap and rebound with feathered headgears waving.

Women with red-painted cheeks and long, braided hair sit in a large half-circle against the willow railing. They, too, join in the singing, and rise to dance with their victorious warriors.

Amid this circular dance arena stands a prisoner bound to a post, haggard with shame and sorrow. He hangs his dishevelled head.

He stares with unseeing eyes upon the bare earth at his feet. With jeers and smirking faces the dancers mock the Dakota captive. Rowdy braves and small boys hoot and yell in derision.

Silent among the noisy mob, a tall woman, leaning both elbows on the round willow railing, peers into the lighted arena. The dancing centre fire shines bright into her handsome face, intensifying the night in her dark eyes. It breaks into myriad points upon her beaded dress. Unmindful of the surging throng jostling her at either side, she glares in upon the hateful, scoffing men. Suddenly she turns her head. Tittering maids whisper near her ear:

"There! There! See him now, sneering in the captive's face. 'Tis he who sprang upon the young man and dragged him by his long hair to yonder post. See! He is handsome! How gracefully he dances!"

The silent young woman looks toward the bound captive. She sees a warrior, scarce older than the captive, flourishing a tomahawk in the Dakota's face. A burning rage darts forth from her eyes and brands him for a victim of revenge. Her heart mutters within her breast, "Come, I wish to meet you, vile foe, who captured my lover and tortures him now with a living death."

Here the singers hush their voices, and the dancers scatter to their various resting-places along the willow ring. The victor gives a reluctant last twirl of his tomahawk, then, like the others, he leaves the centre ground. With head and shoulders swaying from side to side, he carries a high-pointing chin toward the willow railing. Sitting down upon the ground with crossed legs, he fans himself with an outspread turkey wing.

Now and then he stops his haughty blinking to peep out of the corners of his eyes. He hears some one clearing her throat gently. It is unmistakably for his ear. The wing-fan swings irregularly to and fro. At length he turns a proud face over a bare shoulder and beholds a handsome woman smiling.

"Ah, she would speak to a hero!" thumps his heart wildly.

The singers raise their voices in unison. The music is irresistible. Again lunges the victor into the open arena. Again he leers into the captive's face. At every interval between the songs he returns to his resting-place. Here the young woman awaits him. As he approaches she smiles boldly into his eyes. He is pleased with her face and her smile.

Waving his wing-fan spasmodically in front of his face, he sits with his ears pricked up. He catches a low whisper. A hand taps him lightly on the shoulder. The handsome woman speaks to him in his own tongue. "Come out into the night. I wish to tell you who I am."

He must know what sweet words of praise the handsome woman has for him. With both hands he spreads the meshes of the loosely-woven willows, and crawls out unnoticed into the dark.

Before him stands the young woman. Beckoning him with a slender hand, she steps backward, away from the light and the restless throng of onlookers. He follows with impatient strides. She quickens her pace. He lengthens his strides. Then suddenly the woman turns from him and darts away with amazing speed. Clinching his fists and biting his lower lip, the young man runs after the fleeing woman. In his maddened pursuit he forgets the dance arena.

Beside a cluster of low bushes the woman halts. The young man, panting for breath and plunging headlong forward, whispers loud, "Pray tell me, are you a woman or an evil spirit to lure me away?"

Turning on heels firmly planted in the earth, the woman gives a wild spring forward, like a panther for its prey. In a husky voice she hissed between her teeth, "I am a Dakota woman!"

From her unerring long knife the enemy falls heavily at her feet. The Great Spirit heard Tusee's prayer on the hilltop. He gave her a warrior's strong heart to lessen the foe by one.

A bent old woman's figure, with a bundle like a grandchild slung on her back, walks round and round the dance-house. The wearied onlookers are leaving in twos and threes. The tired dancers creep out of the willow railing, and some go out at the entrance way, till the singers, too, rise from the drum and are trudging drowsily homeward. Within the arena the centre fire lies broken in red embers. The night no longer lingers about the willow railing, but, hovering into the dance-house, covers here and there a snoring man whom sleep has overpowered where he sat.

The captive in his tight-binding rawhide ropes hangs in hopeless despair. Close about him the gloom of night is slowly crouching. Yet the last red, crackling embers cast a faint light upon his long black hair, and, shining through the thick mats, caress his wan face with undying hope.

Still about the dance-house the old woman prowls. Now the embers are gray with ashes.

The old bent woman appears at the entrance way. With a cautious, groping foot she enters. Whispering between her teeth a lullaby for her sleeping child in her blanket, she searches for something forgotten.

Noisily snored the dreaming men in the darkest parts. As the lisping old woman draws nigh, the captive again opens his eyes.

A forefinger she presses to her lip. The young man arouses himself from his stupor. His senses belie him. Before his wide-open eyes the old bent figure straightens into its youthful stature. Tusee herself is beside him. With a stroke upward and downward she severs the cruel cords with her sharp blade. Dropping her blanket from her shoulders, so that it hangs from her girdled waist like a skirt, she shakes the large bundle into a light shawl for her lover. Quickly she spreads it over his bare back.

"Come!" she whispers, and turns to go; but the young man, numb and helpless, staggers nigh to falling.

The sight of his weakness makes her strong. A mighty power thrills her body. Stooping beneath his outstretched arms grasping at the air for support, Tusee lifts him upon her broad shoulders. With half-running, triumphant steps she carries him away into the open night.

Charles A. Eastman

Charles Alexander Eastman was born on February 19, 1858, near Redwood Falls, Minnesota. His father, Ite Wakandhi (Many Lightnings), or Jacob Eastman, was a Wahpeton Sioux; his mother, Mary Nancy Eastman, was a mixed-blood, the granddaughter of artist Seth Eastman. Many Lightnings was imprisoned for participating in the Sioux uprising of 1862, and Mary Eastman died shortly after her son's birth. Consequently, Charles Eastman was brought up by his grandmother and uncle in the region of what is now North Dakota and Manitoba. His Sioux name was Ohiyesa (Winner).

During his imprisonment, Many Lightnings converted to Christianity and took the name Jacob Eastman. Upon his release he joined other Sioux to form an Anglo-oriented community named Flandreau. In 1873 he fetched his fifteen-year-old son from Canada and enrolled him at the mission school in Flandreau. Ohiyesa, who had been brought up entirely in a traditional Sioux manner, thereupon became Charles Eastman. He attended the mission school for two years and then transferred to the Santee Normal Training School. In 1876 he entered Beloit College in Wisconsin, where he studied for the next three years. Between 1879 and 1881 he attended Knox College in Illinois and Kimball Union Academy in New Hampshire from 1882 to 1883. He was then awarded a scholarship to Dartmouth, where he graduated in 1887. Finally, he enrolled at the Boston University School of Medicine and earned his M.D. in 1890 at the age of thirty-two. Eastman was undoubtedly one of the most educated Indians of his time and was therefore often held up by progressives as a model.

After his graduation, Eastman accepted a post as a government physician at the Pine Ridge Agency. There he witnessed the aftermath of the massacre at Wounded Knee, treating many of the survivors. In 1891 he married Elaine Goodale, who was the supervisor of education for the Sioux. Two years later he resigned following a dispute with the reservation agent and moved with his wife to St. Paul, where he practiced briefly.

Between 1894 and 1898 he served as a field secretary of the YMCA, during which time he organized some forty local YMCAs for Indians. He was also appointed to represent the Santee in an effort to recover overdue annuity payments, a position that ultimately led to disputes between the tribe and him. Eastman then worked at the Carlisle Indian School for a short period as an outing agent prior to becoming a government physician at the Crow Creek Reservation in South Dakota. In 1903 he again resigned because of disagreements with the local agent. The federal government then hired him to assign anglicized names to the Sioux, a task he had completed by 1908.

By this time Eastman had established a reputation as an author and lecturer. He began his literary career with a number of autobiographical sketches in *St. Nicholas* magazine, having been prompted by his wife, who was to be the chief editor of his future works. These stories appeared collectively under the title *Indian Boyhood* (New York: McClure, Phillips & Co., 1902; reprint, New York: Dover, 1971), and they were soon followed by the publication of two additional collections of short stories, entitled *Red Hunters and the Animal People* (New York: Harper & Bros., 1904; reprint, New York: AMS, 1976) and *Old Indian Days* (New York: McClure Co., 1907; reprint, Rapid City, S.D.: Fenwyn, 1970). Together with his wife he produced a collection of traditional stories, *Wigwam Evenings* (Boston: Little, Brown and Co., 1909). His later publications dealt with traditional and contemporary Indian life and included *The Soul of the Indian* (Boston: Houghton Mifflin Co., 1911; reprint, Lincoln: University of Nebraska Press, 1980), *The Indian To-day: The Past and Future of the First American* (Garden City, N.Y.: Doubleday, Page, and Co., 1915; reprint, New York: AMS, 1975), *From the Deep Woods to Civilization* (Boston: Little, Brown and Co., 1916; reprint, Lincoln: University of Nebraska Press, 1977; his second autobiographical volume), and *Indian Heroes and Great Chieftains* (Boston: Little, Brown and Co., 1918), as well as countless articles.

Charles Eastman actively supported the Boy Scouts, operating his own summer camp for some time and publishing numerous works for the organization, such as *Indian Scout Talks* (Boston: Little, Brown, and Co., 1914). He was also one of the founders of the Society of American Indians, and although his participation in its activities was very sporadic, he occasionally wrote for its journal. In 1911 he represented the North American Indians at the First Universal Races Congress in London. In 1923 he was appointed to the position of U.S. Indian inspector, which he was to hold for nineteen months. That same year he also served as a member of the Committee of One Hundred to investigate Indian policies, which laid the groundwork for the famous 1928 Meriam Report, prepared by the Brookings Institution. He retired for health reasons in 1925 and died on January 8, 1938, in Detroit.

REFERENCES

Copeland, Marion W. *Charles Alexander Eastman (Ohiyesa)*. Boise State University Western Writers Series. Boise, Idaho: Boise State University, 1978).

Miller, David R. "Charles Alexander Eastman, the 'Winner': From Deep Woods to Civilization." In Margot Liberty, ed., *American Indian Intellectuals*, 67–73. Proceedings of the American Ethnological Society, 1976. St. Paul: West Publishing Company, 1978.

Schöler, Bo. "Images and Counter-Images: Ohiyesa, Standing Bear and American Literature." *American Indian Culture and Research Journal* 5 (1981): 37–62.

Stensland, Anna L. "Charles Alexander Eastman: Sioux Storyteller and Historian." *American Indian Quarterly* 3 (Fall 1977): 199–208.

Wilson, Raymond. "The Writings of Ohiyesa—Charles Alexander Eastman, M.D., Santee Sioux." *South Dakota History* 6 (Winter 1975): 55–73.

———. *Ohiyesa: Charles Eastman, Santee Sioux*. Urbana: University of Illinois Press, 1983.

STORIES BY CHARLES A. EASTMAN

"Hakadah's First Offering." *Current Literature* 34 (January 1903): 29–32.

"The Great Cat's Nursery." *Harper's Monthly*, November 1903, 939–946.

"The Gray Chieftain." *Harper's Monthly*, March 1904, 882–887. Reprinted in William Dean Howells and Henry Mills Alden, eds., *Under the Sunset* (New York: Harper & Brothers, 1906).

"The Mustering of the Herds." *Out West*, November 1904, 439–445.

"The Madness of Bald Eagle." *Southern Workman* 34 (March 1905): 141–143.

"Grave of the Dog." *Metropolitan Magazine*, Feb. 1906, 569.

"War Maiden of the Sioux." *Ladies Home Journal*, August 1906, 14.

"The Singing Spirit." *Sunset*, December 1907, 112–121.

The Gray Chieftain

OHIYESA [CHARLES A. EASTMAN, M.D.]

On the westernmost verge of the Cedar Butte stood Haykinskah and his mate. They looked steadily toward the setting sun, over a landscape which up to that time had scarcely been viewed by man —the inner circle of the Bad Lands.

Cedar Butte guards the southeastern entrance of that wonderland, standing fully a thousand feet above the surrounding country, and nearly half a mile long by a quarter of a mile wide. The summit is a level, grassy plain, its edges heavily fringed with venerable cedars. To attempt the ascent of this butte is like trying to scale the walls of Babylon, for its sides are high and all but inaccessible. Near the top there are hanging lands or terraces and innumerable precipitous points, with here and there deep chimneys or abysses in the solid rock. There are many hidden recesses, and more than one secret entrance to this ancient castle of the Gray Chieftain and his ancestors, but to assail it successfully required more than common skill and spirit.

Many a coyote had gone up as high as the second leaping bridge, and there abandoned the attempt. Old Grizzly had once or twice begun the ascent with doubt and misgiving, but soon discovered his mistake, and made clumsy haste to descend before he should tumble into an abyss from which no one ever returns. Only Igmutanka, the mountain lion, had achieved the summit, and at every ascent he had been well repaid; yet even he seldom chose to risk such a climb, when there were many fine hunting-grounds in safer neighborhoods.

So it was that Cedar Butte had been the peaceful home of the Big Spoonhorns for untold ages. To be sure, some of the younger and more adventurous members of the clan would depart from time to time to found new families, but the wiser and more conservative were content to remain in their stronghold. There stood the two patriarchs, looking down complacently upon the herds of buffalo, antelope, and elk that peopled the lower plains. While the red sun hovered over the western hills, a coyote upon a nearby eminence gave his accustomed call to his mate. This served as a signal to all the wild hunters of the plains to set up their inharmonious evening serenade, to which the herbivorous kindred paid but little attention. The phlegmatic Spoonhorn pair listened to it all with a fine air of indifference, like that of one who sits upon his own balcony, superior to the passing noises of the street.

It was a charming moonlight night upon the cedar-fringed plain, and there the old chief presently joined the others in feast and play. His mate sought out a secret resting-place. She followed the next gulch, which was a perfect labyrinth of caves and pockets, and after leaping two chasms she reached her favorite spot. Here the gulch made a square turn, affording a fine view of the country through a windowlike opening. Above and below this were perpendicular walls, and at the bottom a small cavity—the washout made by a root of a pine which had long since fallen. To this led a narrow terrace —so narrow that man or beast would stop and hesitate long before making the venture. The place was her own by right of daring and discovery, and the mother's instinct had brought her here tonight.

In a little while relief came, and the ewe stood over a new-born lamb, licking tenderly the damp, silky coat of hair, and trimming the little hoofs of their cartilaginous points. The world was quiet now, and those whose business it was to hunt or feed at night must do so in silence, for such is the law of the plains. The wearied mother slept in peace.

The sun was well above the butte when she awoke, although it was cool and shadowy still in her concealed abode. She gave suck to the lamb, and caressed it for some time before she reluctantly prepared its cradle according to the custom of her people. She made a little pocket in the floor of the cave and gently put the baby in. Then she covered him all up, save the nose and eyes, with dry soil. She put her nose to his little sensitive ear and breathed into it warm love and caution, and he felt and understood that he must keep his eyes closed and breathe gently, lest bear or wolf or man should catch his big eyes or hear his breathing if they should find her trail. Again she put her warm, loving nose to his eyes, she patted a little more earth on his body and smoothed it off. The tachinchana closed his eyes in obedience, and she left him for the plain above, in search of food and sunlight.

At a little before dawn two wild hunters left their camp and set out for the Cedar Butte. Their movements were marked by unusual care and secrecy. Presently they hid their ponies in a deep ravine and groped their way up through the difficult Bad Lands, now and then pausing to listen. The two were close friends and rival hunters of their tribe.

"I think, friend, you have mistaken the haunts of the Spoonhorn," remarked Grayfoot, as the pair came out upon one of the lower terraces. He said this rather to test his friend, for it was their habit thus to criticize and question one another's judgment, in order to extract from each other fresh observations. What the one did not know about the habits of the animals they hunted in common, the other could usually supply.

"This is his home. I know it," replied Wahye. "And in this thing the animals are much like ourselves. They will not leave an old haunt unless forced to do so, either by lack of food or overwhelming danger."

They had already passed on to the next terrace and leaped a deep chasm to gain the opposite side of the butte, when Grayfoot suddenly whispered, "Inajin!" (Stop!). Both men listened attentively. "Tap, tap, tap," an almost metallic sound came to them from around the perpendicular wall of rock.

"He is chipping his horns," exclaimed the hunter, overjoyed to surprise the chieftain at this his secret occupation. "Poor beast! they are now too long for him, so that he cannot reach the short grass to feed. Some of them die starving, when they have not the strength to do the hard bucking against the rock to shorten their horns. He chooses this time, when he thinks no one will hear him, and he even leaves his own clan when it is necessary for him to do this. Come, let us crawl upon him unawares!"

They proceeded cautiously and with catlike steps around the next projection, and stood upon a narrow strip of slanting terrace. At short intervals the pounding noise continued, but, strain their eyes as they might, they could see nothing. Yet they knew that a few paces from them, in the darkness, the old chief was painfully driving his massive horns against the solid rock. So they lay flat upon the ground under a dead cedar, whose trunk and the color of the scanty soil resembled their clothing, and on their heads they had stuck some bunches of sage-bush, to conceal them from the eyes of the Spoonhorn.

With the first gray of the approaching dawn the two hunters looked eagerly about them. There, in all his majesty, heightened by the wild grandeur of his surroundings, stood the Gray Chieftain of the Cedar Butte! He had no thought of being observed at that hour. Entirely unsuspicious of danger, he stood alone upon a pedestal-like terrace, from which vantage-point it was his wont to survey the surrounding country every morning. If the secret must be told, he had done so for years, ever since he became the head chief of the Cedar Butte clan.

It is the custom of their tribe that when a ram attains the age of five years he is entitled to a clan of his own. He must thereafter defend his right and supremacy against all comers. His experience and knowledge are the guide of his clan. In view of all this, the Gray Chieftain had been very thorough in his observations. There was not an object anywhere near the shape of bear, wolf, or man for miles around his kingdom upon Hanta Pahah that was not noted, as well as the relative positions of rocks and conspicuous trees.

The best time for Haykinskah to make his daily observations is at sunrise and sunset, when the air is usually clear and objects appear distinct. Between these times the clan feed and settle down to chew their cud and sleep; yet some are always on the alert to catch a passing stranger within their field of observation. But the old chief Spoonhorn pays very little attention. He may be nestled in a gulch just big enough to hold him, either sound asleep or leisurely chewing his cud. The younger members of the clan take their position upon the upper terraces of the great and almost inaccessible butte, under the shade of its projecting rocks, after a whole night's feasting and play upon the plain.

As Spoonhorn stood motionless, looking away off toward the distant hills, the plain below appeared from this elevated point very smooth and sheetlike, and every moving object a mere speck. His form and color were not very different from the dirty gray rocks and clay of the butte.

Wahye broke the silence: "I know of no animal that stands so long without movement, unless it is the turtle. I think he is the largest ram I have ever seen."

"I am sure he did not chip where he stands now," remarked Grayfoot. "This chipping-place is a monastery to the priests of the Spoonhorn tribe. It is their medicine-man's lodge. I have more than once approached the spot, but could never find the secret entrance."

"Shall I shoot him now?" whispered his partner in the chase.

"No, do not do it. He is a real chief. He looks mysterious and noble. Let us learn to know him better. Besides, if we kill him we will never see him again. Look; he will fall to that deep gulch ten trees' length below, where no one can get at him."

As Grayfoot spoke, the animal shifted his position, facing them squarely. The two men closed their eyes and wrinkled their motionless faces into the semblance of two lifeless mummies. The old sage of the mountains was apparently deceived; but after a few moments he got down from his lofty position and disappeared around a point of rock.

"I never care to shoot an animal while he is giving me a chance to know his ways," explained Grayfoot. "We have plenty of buffalo meat. We are not hungry. All we want is spoons. We can get one or two sheep by and by, if we have more wit than they."

To this speech Wahye agreed, for his curiosity was now fully aroused by Grayfoot's view, although he had never before thought of it in that way. It had always been the desire for meat that had chiefly moved him in the matter of the hunt.

Having readjusted their sage wigs, the hunters made the circuit of the abyss that divided them from the ram, and as they looked for his trail, they noticed the tracks of a large ewe leading down toward the inaccessible gulches.

"Ah! she has some secret down there. She never leaves her clan like this, unless it is to steal away for a personal affair of her own."

So saying, Grayfoot and his fellow tracked the ewe's footprint along the verge of a deep gulch with much trouble and patience. The hunter's curiosity and a strong desire to know her secret impelled the former to lead the way.

"What will be our profit if one slips and goes down into the gulch, never to be seen again?" remarked Wahye, as they approached a leaping-place. The chasm below was of a great depth and dark. "It is not wise for us to follow farther; this ewe has no horns that can be made into spoons."

"Come, friend, it is when one is doubting that mishaps are apt to occur," urged his companion.

"Koda, heyu yo!" exclaimed Wahye the next moment in distress.

"Hehehe, koda! hold fast!" cried the other.

Wahye's moccasined foot had slipped on the narrow trail, and in the twinkling of an eye he had almost gone down a precipice of a hundred feet; but by a desperate launch forward he caught the bough of an overhanging cedar and swung by his hands over the abyss.

Quickly Grayfoot pulled both their bows from the quivers. He first tied himself to the trunk of the cedar with his packing-strap, which always hung from his belt. Then he held both the bows toward his friend, who, not without difficulty, changed his hold from the cedar bough to the bows. After a short but determined effort the two men stood side by side once more upon the narrow foothold of the terrace. Without a word they followed the ewe's track to the cave.

Here she had lain last night! Both men began to search for other marks, but they found not so much as a sign of scratching anywhere. They examined the ground closely, but without success. All at once a faint "ba-a-a" came from almost under their feet. They saw a puff of smokelike dust as the little creature called for its mother. It had felt the footsteps of the hunters, and mistaken them for those of its own folk.

Wahye hastily dug into the place with his hands and found the soil loose. Soon he uncovered the little lamb. "Ba-a-a," it cried again, and quick as a flash the ewe appeared, stamping the ground in wrath.

Wahye seized an arrow and fitted it to the string, but his companion checked him. "No, no, my friend. It is not the skin or meat that we are looking for. We want horn for ladles and spoons. The mother is right. We must let her babe alone."

The wild hunters silently retreated, and the ewe ran swiftly to the spot and took her lamb away.

"So it is," said Grayfoot, after a long silence, "all the tribes of earth have some common feeling. I believe they are people as much as we are. The Great Mystery has made them what they are. Although they do not speak our tongue, we seem to understand their thought. It is not right to take the life of any of them unless necessity compels us to do so.

"You know," he continued, "the ewe conceals her lamb in this way until she has trained it to escape from its enemies by leaping up or down from terrace to terrace. I have seen her teaching the yearlings and two-year-olds to dive down the face of a cliff which was fully twice the height of a man. They strike on the head and the two forefeet. The ram falls largely upon his horns, which are curved in such a way as to protect them from injury. The body rebounds slightly, and they get upon their feet as easily as if they had struck a pillow. At first the yearlings hesitate and almost lose their balance, but the mother makes them repeat the performance until they have accomplished it to her satisfaction.

"They are then trained to leap chasms on all fours, and finally the upward jump, which is a more difficult feat. If the height is not great they can clear it neatly, but if it is too high for that, they will catch the rocky ledge with their forefeet and pull themselves up like a man.

"In assisting their young to gain upper terraces they show much ingenuity. I once saw them make a ladder of their bodies. The biggest ram stood braced against the steep wall as high as his body could reach, head placed between his forefeet, while the next biggest one rode his hind parts, and so on until the little ones could walk upon their broad backs to the top. We know that all animals make their young ones practise such feats as are necessary to their safety and advantage, and thus it is that these people are so well fitted to their peculiar mode of life.

"How often we are outwitted by the animals we hunt! The Great

Mystery gives them this chance to save their lives by eluding the hunter, when they have no weapons of defense. The ewe has seen us, and she has doubtless warned all the clan of danger."

But there was one that she did not see! When the old chief left his clan to go to the secret place for chipping his horns, the place where many a past monarch of the Bad Lands has performed that painful operation, he did not intend to rejoin them immediately. It was customary with him at that time to seek solitude and sleep.

The two hunters found and carefully examined the tracks of the fleeing clan. The old ram was not among them. As they followed the trail along the terrace they came to a leaping-place which did not appear to be generally used. Grayfoot stopped and kneeled down to scrutinize the ground below. "Ho!" he exclaimed, "the old chief has gone down this trail, but has not returned. He is lying down near his chipping-place, if there is no other outlet from there."

Both leaped to the next terrace below, and followed the secret pass into a rocky amphitheatre, opening out from the terrace upon which they had first seen the old ram. Here he lay asleep.

Wahye pulled an arrow from his quiver.

"Yes," said his friend, "shoot now! A warrior is always a warrior —and we are looking for horn for spoons!"

The old chief awoke to behold the most dreaded hunter—man— upon the very threshold of his sanctuary! Wildly he sprang upward to gain the top of the cliff. But Wahye was expert and quick in the use of his weapon. He had sent into his side a shaft that was deadly. The monarch's forehoofs caught the edge—he struggled bravely for a moment, then fell limply to the floor below.

"He is dead. My friend, the noblest of chiefs is dead!" exclaimed Grayfoot as he stood over him, in great admiration and respect for the Gray Chieftain.

The Singing Spirit

CHARLES A. EASTMAN [OHIYESA]

I

"Ho, my steed, we must climb one more hill! My reputation depends upon my report!"

Anookasan addressed his pony as if he were a human companion urged on like himself by human need and human ambition. And yet in his heart he had very little hope of sighting any buffalo in that region at just that time of the year.

The Yankton Sioux were ordinarily the most far-sighted of their people in selecting a winter camp, but this year the late fall had caught them rather far east of the Missouri bottoms, their favorite camping-ground. The upper Jim river, called by the Sioux the River of the Gray Woods, was usually bare of large game at that season. Their store of jerked buffalo meat did not hold out as they had hoped, and by March it became an urgent necessity to send out scouts for buffalo.

The old men at the tiyó teepee (council lodge) held a long council. It was decided to select ten of their bravest and hardiest young men to explore the country within three days' journey of their camp.

"Anookasan, uyeyo-o-o, woo, woo!" Thus the ten men were summoned to the council lodge early in the evening to receive their commission. Anookasan was the first called and first to cross the circle of the teepees. A young man of some thirty years, of the original native type, his massive form was wrapped in a fine buffalo robe with the hair inside. He wore a stately eagle feather in his scalp-lock, but no paint about his face. As he entered the lodge, all the inmates greeted him with marked respect, and he was given the place of honor. When all were seated, the great drum was struck and a song sung by four deep-chested men. This was the prelude to a peculiar ceremony.

A large red pipe, which had been filled and laid carefully upon the central hearth, was now taken up by an old man, whose face was painted red. First he held it to the ground with the words "Great Mother, partake of this!" Then he held it toward the sky, saying, "Great Father, smoke this!" Finally he lighted it, took four puffs, pointing it to the four corners of the earth in turn, and finally presented it to Anookasan. This was the oath of office, administered by the chief of the council lodge. The other nine were similarly commissioned, and all accepted the appointment.

It was no light task that was thus religiously enjoined upon these ten men. It meant at the least several days and nights wandering in search of signs of the wily buffalo. It was a public duty and a personal one as well; one that must involve untold hardship, and if overtaken by storm the messengers were in peril of death.

Anookasan returned to his teepee with some misgiving. His old horse, which had so often carried him to victory, was not so strong as he had been in his prime. As his master approached the lodge, the horse welcomed him with a gentle whinny. He was always tethered nearby, ready for any emergency.

"Ah, Wakan, we are once more called upon to do duty! We shall set out before daybreak."

As he spoke, he pushed nearer a few strips of the poplar bark, which was oats to the Indian pony of the olden time.

Anookasan had his extra pair of buffalo-skin moccasins with the hair inside, and his scanty provision of dried meat neatly done up in a small packet and fastened to his saddle. With his companions he started northward up the river of the Gray Woods; five went on the east side and five on the west.

The party had separated each morning, so as to cover as much ground as possible, having agreed to return at night to the river. It was now the third day; their food was all but gone; their horses much worn, and the signs seemed to indicate a storm. Yet the hunger of their friends and their own pride impelled them to persist, for out of many young men they had been chosen, therefore they must prove themselves equal to the occasion.

The sun, now well toward the western horizon, cast over snow-covered plains a purplish light. No living creature was in sight and the quest seemed hopeless, but Anookasan was not one to accept defeat.

"There may be an outlook from yonder hill which will turn failure into success," he thought, as he dug his heels into the sides of his faithful nag. At the same time, he started a "Strong Heart" song to keep his courage up.

At the summit of the ascent he paused and gazed steadily before him. At the foot of the next coteau, he beheld a strip of black. He strained his eyes to look, for the sun had already set behind the hilltops. It was a great herd of buffalo, he thought, which was grazing on the foothills.

"Hi, hi, uncheédah! Hi, hi, tunkásheedah!" he was about to exclaim in gratitude, when looking more closely he discovered his mistake. The dark patch was only timber.

His horse could not carry him any farther, so he got off and ran behind him toward the river. At dusk he hailed his companions.

"Ho, what success?" one cried.

"Not a sign of even a lone bull," replied another.

"Yet I saw a gray wolf going north this evening. His direction is propitious," remarked Anookasan, as he led the others down the slope and into a heavy timber. The river just here made a sharp turn, forming a densely wooded semi-circle, in the shelter of a high bluff.

The braves were all down-hearted because of their ill-luck, and only the sanguine spirit of Anookasan kept them from utter discouragement. Their slight repast had been taken and each man had provided himself with abundance of dry grass and twigs for a bed. They had built a temporary wigwam of the same material, in the center of which there was a generous fire. Each man stretched himself out upon his robe in the glow of it. Anookasan filled the red pipe, and having lighted it he took one or two hasty puffs and held it up to the moon which was scarcely visible behind the cold clouds.

"Great Mother, partake of this smoke! May I eat meat to-morrow!" he exclaimed with solemnity. Having uttered this prayer, he handed the pipe to the man nearest him.

For a time they all smoked in silence; then came a distant call. "Ah, it is Shunkmanito, the wolf! There is something cheering in his voice tonight," declared Anookasan. "Yes, I am sure he is telling us not to be discouraged. You know that the wolf is one of our best friends in trouble. Many a one has been guided back to his home by him in a blizzard, or led to game when in desperate need. My friends, let us not turn back in the morning. Let us go north one more day!"

No one answered immediately, and again silence reigned while one by one they pulled the reluctant whiffs of smoke through the long stem of the calumet.

"What is that?" said one of the men, and all listened intently to catch the delicate sound. They were familiar with all the noises of the night and voices of the forest, but this was not like any of them.

"It sounds like the song of a mosquito, and one might forget while he listens that this is not midsummer," said one.

"I hear also the medicine-man's single drum-beat," suggested another.

"There is a tradition," remarked Anookasan, "that many years ago a party of hunters went up the river on a scout like this of ours. They never returned. Afterward, in the summer, their bones were found near the home of a strange creature, said to be a little man, but he had hair all over him. The Isantees call him Chanótedah. Our old men give him the name Oglúgechana. This singular being is said to be no larger than a newborn babe. He speaks an unknown tongue.

"The home of Oglúgechana is usually a hollow stump, around which all of the nearest trees are felled by lightning. There is an open spot in the deep woods wherever he dwells. His weapons are the plumes of various birds. Great numbers of these variegated feathers are to be found in the deserted lodge of the little man.

"It is told by the old men that Oglúgechana has a weird music by which he sometimes bewitches lone travelers. He leads them hither and thither about his place until they have lost their senses. Then he speaks to them. He may make of them great war prophets or medicine men, but his commands are hard to fulfill. If any one sees him and comes away before he is bewildered, the man dies as soon as he smells the camp-fire, or when he enters his home his nearest relative dies suddenly."

The warrior who related this legend assumed the air of one who narrates authentic history, and his listeners appeared to be seriously impressed. What we call the supernatural was as real to them as any part of their lives.

"This thing does not stop to breathe at all. His music seems to go on endlessly," said one, with considerable uneasiness.

"It comes from the heavy timber north of us, under the high cliff," reported a warrior who had stepped outside of the rude temporary structure to inform himself more clearly of the direction of the sound.

"Anookasan, you are our leader—tell us what we should do! We will follow you. I believe we ought to leave this spot immediately. This is perhaps the spirit of some dead enemy," suggested another. Meanwhile the red pipe was refilled and sent around the circle to calm their disturbed spirits.

When the calumet returned at last to the one addressed, he took it in a preoccupied manner and spoke between labored pulls on the stem.

"I am just like yourselves—nothing more than flesh—with a spirit that is as ready to leave me as water to run from a punctured waterbag! When we think thus, we are weak. Let us rather think upon the brave deeds of our ancestors! This singing spirit has a gentle voice, I am ready to follow and learn if it be an enemy or no. Let us all be found together next summer if need be!"

"Ho, ho, ho!" was the full-throated response.

"All put on your war paint," suggested Anookasan. "Have your knives and arrows ready!"

They did so, and all stole silently through the black forest in the direction of the mysterious sound. Clearer and clearer it came through the frosty air, but it was a foreign sound to the savage ear. Now it seemed to them almost like a distant waterfall; then it recalled the low hum of summer insects and the drowsy drone of the bumble bee. Thump, thump, thump! was the regular accompaniment.

Nearer and nearer to the cliff they came, deeper into the wild heart of the woods. At last out of the gray formless night a dark shape appeared! It looked to them like a huge buffalo bull standing motionless in the forest, and from his throat there apparently proceeded the thump of the medicine drum, and the song of the beguiling spirit.

All of a sudden, a spark went up into the air. As they continued to approach, there became visible a deep glow about the middle of the dark object. Whatever it was, they had never heard of anything like it in all their lives.

Anookasan was a little in advance of his companions, and it was he who finally discovered a wall of logs laid one upon another. Half way up there seemed to be stretched a *par-fleche* (raw-hide) from which a dim light emanated. He still thought of Oglúgechana, who dwells within a hollow tree, and determined to surprise and if possible to overpower this wonder-working old man.

All now took their knives in their hands and advanced with their leader to the attack upon the log hut. "Wa-wa-wa-wa, woo, woo!" they cried. Zip! zip! went the *par-fleche* door and window, and they all rushed in.

There sat a man upon a roughly hewn stool. He was attired in wolf skins and wore a fox skin cap upon his head. The larger portion of his face was clothed with natural fur. A rudely made cedar fiddle was tucked under his furred chin. Supporting it with his left hand, he sawed it vigorously with a bow that was not unlike an Indian boy's miniature weapon, while his moccasined left foot came down upon the sod floor in time with the music. When the shrill warwhoop came, and the door and window were cut in strips by the knives of the Indians, he did not even cease playing, but instinctively he closed his eyes, so as not to behold the horror of his own end.

I I

It was long ago, upon the rolling prairie south of the Devil's Lake, that a motley body of hunters gathered near a mighty herd of the bison, in the Moon of Falling Leaves. These were the first generation of the Canadian mixed-bloods, who sprang up in such numbers as to form almost new people. These semi-wild Americans soon became a necessity to the Hudson Bay Company, as they were the greatest hunters of the bison, and made more use of this wonderful animal than even their aboriginal ancestors.

A curious race of people this in their make-up and their customs! Their shaggy black hair was allowed to grow long, reaching to the broad shoulders, then cut off abruptly, making their heads look like a thatched house. Their dark faces were in most cases well covered with hair, their teeth large and white, and their eyes usually liquid black, although occasionally one had a tiger-brown or cold gray eye. Their costume was a buckskin shirt with abundance of fringes, buckskin pantaloons with short leggings, a gay sash, and a cap of fox fur. Their arms consisted of flint-lock guns, hatchets and butcher knives. Their ponies were small, but as hardy as themselves.

As these men gathered in the neighborhood of an immense herd of buffalo, they busied themselves in adjusting the girths of their beautifully beaded, pillow-like saddles. Among them there were exceptional riders and hunters. It was said that few could equal Antoine Michaud in feats of riding into and through the herd. There he stood, all alone, the observed of many others. It was his habit to give several Indian yells when the onset began so as to insure a successful hunt.

In this instance, Antoine gave his usual whoops, and when they had almost reached the herd, he lifted his flint-lock over his head and plunged into the black, moving mass. With a sound like the distant rumbling of thunder, those tens of thousands of buffalo hoofs were pounding the earth in retreat. Thus Antoine disappeared.

His wild steed dashed into the midst of the vast herd. Fortunately for him, the animals kept clear of him; but alas! the gap through which he had entered instantly closed again.

He yelled frantically to secure an outlet, but without effect. He had tied a red bandanna around his head to keep the hair off his face, and he now took this off and swung it crazily about him to scatter the buffalo, but it availed him nothing.

With such a mighty herd in flight, the speed could not be great; therefore the "Bois Brule" settled himself to the situation, allowing his pony to canter along slowly to save his strength. It required much tact and presence of mind to keep an open space, for the few paces of obstruction behind had gradually grown into a mile.

The mighty host moved continually southward, walking and running alternately. As the sun neared the western horizon, it fired the sky above them, and all the distant hills and prairies were in the glow of it, but immediately about them was a thick cloud of dust, and the ground appeared like a fire-swept plain.

Suddenly Antoine was aware of a tremendous push from behind. The animals smelled the cool water of a spring which formed a large bog in the midst of the plain. This solitary pond or marsh was a watering place for the wild animals. All pushed and edged toward it; it was impossible for any one to withstand the combined strength of so many.

Antoine and his steed were in imminent danger of being pushed into the mire and trampled upon, but a mere chance brought them upon solid ground. As they were crowded across the marsh, his pony drank heartily, and he, for the first time, let go his bridle, put his two palms together for a dipper, and drank greedily of the bitter water. He had not eaten since early morning, so he now pulled up some bullrushes and ate of the tender bulbs, while the pony grazed as best he could on the tops of the tall grass.

It was now dark. The night was well-nigh intolerable for Antoine. The buffalo were about him in countless numbers, regarding him with vicious glances. It was only by reason of the natural offensiveness of man that they gave him any space. The bellowing of the bulls became general, and there was a marked uneasiness on the part of the herd. This was a sign of approaching storm, therefore the unfortunate hunter had this additional cause for anxiety. Upon the western horizon were seen flashes of lightning.

The cloud which had been a mere speck upon the horizon had now increased to large proportions. Suddenly the wind came, and lightning flashes became more frequent, showing the ungainly forms of the animals like strange monsters in the white light. The colossal herd was again in violent motion. It was a blind rush for shelter, and no heed was paid to buffalo wallows or even deep gulches. All was in the deepest of darkness. There seemed to be groaning in heaven and earth—millions of hoofs and throats roaring in unison.

As a shipwrecked man clings to a mere fragment of wood, so Antoine, although almost exhausted with fatigue, still stuck to the saddle of his equally plucky pony. Death was imminent for them both. As the mad rush continued, every flash displayed heaps of bison in death struggle under the hoofs of their companions. From time to time Antoine crossed himself and whispered a prayer to the Virgin, and again he spoke to his horse after the fashion of an Indian:

"Be brave, be strong, my horse! If we survive this trial, you shall have great honor!"

The stampede continued until they reached the bottom lands, and like a rushing stream, their course was turned aside by the steep bank of a creek or small river. Then they moved more slowly in wide sweeps or circles, until the storm ceased, and the exhausted hunter, still in his saddle, took some snatches of sleep.

When he awoke and looked about him again it was morning. The herd had entered the strip of timber which lay on both sides of the river, and it was here that Antoine conceived his first distinct hope of saving himself.

"Waw, waw, waw!" was the hoarse cry that came to his ears, apparently from a human being in distress. Antoine strained his eyes and craned his neck to see who it could be. Through an opening in the branches ahead he perceived a large grizzly bear lying along an inclined limb and hugging it desperately to maintain his position. The herd had now thoroughly pervaded the timber, and the bear was likewise hemmed in. He had taken to his unaccustomed refuge after making a brave stand against several bulls, one of which lay dead near by, while he himself was bleeding from many wounds.

Antoine had been assiduously looking for a friendly tree, by means of which he hoped to effect his escape from captivity by the army of bison. His horse, by chance, made his way directly under the very box-elder that was sustaining the bear and there was a convenient branch just within his reach. The Bois Brule was not then in an aggressive mood, and he saw at a glance that the occupant of the tree would not interfere with him. They were, in fact, companions in distress. Antoine tried to give a war whoop as he sprang desperately from the pony's back and seized the cross-limb with both his hands.

The hunter dangled in the air for a minute that to him seemed a year. Then he gathered up all the strength that was in him and with one grand effort he pulled himself upon the limb. If he had failed in this, he would have fallen to the ground under the hoofs of the buffalo, and been at their mercy.

After he had adjusted his seat as comfortably as he could, Antoine surveyed the situation. He had at least escaped from sudden and certain death. It grieved him that he had been forced to abandon his horse, and he had no idea how far he had come nor any means of returning to his friends, who had, no doubt, given him up for lost. His immediate needs were rest and food.

Accordingly he selected a fat cow and emptied into her sides one barrel of his gun, which had been slung across his chest. He went on shooting until he had killed many fat cows, greatly to the discomfiture of his neighbor, the bear, while the bison vainly struggled among themselves to keep the fatal spot clear.

By the middle of the afternoon the main body of the herd had passed, and Antoine was sure that his captivity had at last come to an end. Then he swung himself from his limb to the ground, and walked stiffly to the carcass of the nearest cow, which he dressed, and prepared himself a meal. But first he took a piece of liver on a long pole to the bear!

Antoine finally decided to settle in the recesses of the heavy timber for the winter, as he was on foot and alone, and not able to travel any great distance. He jerked the meat of all the animals he had killed, and prepared their skins for bedding and clothing. The Bois Brule and Ami, as he called the bear, soon became necessary to one another. The former considered the bear very good company, and the latter had learned that man's business, after all, is not to kill every animal he meets. He had been fed and kindly treated when helpless from his wounds, and this he could not forget.

Antoine was soon busy erecting a small log hut, while the other partner kept a sharp lookout, and after his hurts were healed, often brought in some small game. The two had a perfect understanding without many words; at least, the speech was all upon one side. In his leisure moments, Antoine had occupied himself with whittling out a rude fiddle of cedar wood, strung with the guts of a wildcat that he had killed. Every evening that winter he would sit down after supper and play all the old familiar pieces, varied with improvisations of his own. At first, the music and the incessant pounding time with his foot annoyed the bear. At times, too, the Canadian would call out the figures for the dance. All this Ami became accustomed to in time, and even showed no small interest in the buzzing of the little cedar box. Not infrequently, he was out in the evening, and the human partner was left alone. It chanced, quite fortunately, that the bear was absent on the night that the red folk rudely invaded the lonely hut.

The calmness of the strange being had stayed their hands. They had never before seen a man of other race than their own!

"Is this Chanótedah? Is he man, or beast?" the warriors asked one another.

"Ho, wake up, koda!" exclaimed Anookasan. "Maybe he is of the porcupine tribe, ashamed to look at us, as that animal hides his face when he meets with a stranger!"

At this moment they spied the haunch of venison which swung from a cross-stick over a fine bed of coals, in front of the rude mud chimney.

"Ho, koda has something to eat! Sit down, sit down!" they shouted to one another.

Now Antoine opened his eyes for the first time upon his unlooked-for guests. They were a haggard and hungry-looking set. Anookasan extended his hand, and Antoine gave it a hearty shake. He set his fiddle against the wall and began to cut up the smoking venison into generous pieces and place it before them. All ate like famished men, while the firelight intensified the red paint upon their faces.

When he had satisfied his first hunger, Anookasan spoke in signs. "Friend, we have never before heard a song like that of your little cedar box. We had supposed it to be a spirit, or some harmful thing, hence our attack upon it. We never saw any people of your sort. What is your tribe?"

Antoine explained his plight in the same manner, and the two soon came to an understanding. The Canadian told the starving hunters of a buffalo herd a little way to the north, and one of their number was dispatched homeward with the news. In two days, the entire band reached Antoine's place. The Bois Brule was treated with kindness and honor, and the tribe gave him a wife. Suffice it to say that Antoine lived and died among the Yanktons but Ami could not brook the invasion upon their hermit life. He was never seen after that first evening.

Alexander Posey

Alexander Lawrence Posey was born on August 3, 1873, in Creek Nation territory near the present town of Eufaula, Oklahoma. His father, Lewis H. Posey, was of Scotch-Irish descent, and his mother, Pohas Harjo, or Nancy Phillips, was a full-blood Creek. Posey grew up bilingually, receiving instruction in English from his father and a private tutor. He attended school at Eufaula and in 1890 enrolled at Bacone University in Muskogee, where he studied for five years. He began to write while at Bacone, publishing his earliest poems in the 1892 issue of the *Bacone Indian University Instructor*.

Following his graduation in 1895 he was elected to a seat in the House of Warriors, the lower chamber of the Creek legislature. A year later he was appointed superintendent of the Creek Nation Orphan Asylum at Okmulgee, from which post he resigned in 1897. He also served briefly as the superintendent of public instruction of the Creek Nation prior to taking up farming on his land near Stidham. It was while he lived on his farm that he wrote most of his poems, published posthumously by his wife, Minnie Harris (*The Poems of Alexander Lawrence Posey* [Topeka, Kans.: Crane & Co., 1910]). Later, Posey was appointed superintendent of the National High School at Eufaula and the Wetumka National School. In 1902 and 1903 he edited the Eufaula *Indian Journal*. At this time the Dawes Act was beginning to affect the Five Civilized Tribes, and he made its effects the main subject of his Fus Fixico letters. In 1903 he became editor of the *Muskogee Times* for a brief period and then assumed charge of the Creek Enrollment Field Party of the Five Civilized Tribes at the request of the Dawes Commission. His duty was to appraise the land held by the tribes in preparation for determining allotments. Afterward, he resumed editing the *Indian*

Journal, for which he wrote numerous articles and "letters" on local events. He died in a drowning accident on May 27, 1908.

REFERENCES

Arrington, Ruth. "Alex Posey: Creek Statesman, Journalist, and Poet." In George E. Carter and James R. Parker, eds., *Essays in Minority Folklore,* 77–87. Selected Proceedings of the 3rd Annual Conference on Minority Studies, 1975. La Crosse: Institute for Minority Studies, University of Wisconsin-La Crosse, 1977.

Challacombe, Doris. "Alexander Lawrence Posey." *Chronicles of Oklahoma* 11 (December 1933): 1010–1018.

Posey, Alexander. "The Journal of Alexander Lawrence Posey, January 1 to September 4, 1897." *Chronicles of Oklahoma* 45 (Winter 1967–1968): 393–432. Experiences as superintendent of the Creek Nation Orphan Asylum at Okmulgee, Oklahoma.

———. "Journal of the Creek Enrollment Field Party, 1905." *Chronicles of Oklahoma* 46 (Spring 1968): 2–19.

Alexander Posey's Fus Fixico letters are too numerous to list here. See Daniel Littlefield and James Parins, comps., *A Bio-Bibliography of Native American Writers, 1772–1924* (Metuchen, N.J.: Scarecrow Press, 1981). Many of the letters are in the Mitchell Collection, Western History Collections, University of Oklahoma Library.

Letter of Fus Fixico, March 23, 1906

ALEXANDER POSEY

"Well, so," Hotgun he say, "if we didn't get statehood this spring, we could had poke greens an' wild onions scrambled with eggs, anyhow."

An' Tookpafka Micco he spit back in the corner o' the fire place and say, "Well, maybe so, we have greens an' statehood both. The young hoosier statesman from the banks o' the Wabash was made a big spread eagle talk in the senate chamber an created a stir in the galleries an' lobby halls, an' politicians was hurryin' back from the capital like bees swarmin' an' workin' overtime. So it didn't take a firstclass prophet to prophesy 'bout statehood, an' you didn't had to put on your specs to see which way the wind was blowin' the straw."

Wolf Warrior an' Kono Harjo grunt like they didn't welcome the news an' shake they heads like they thought the Injin was fall on evil days.

Then Hotgun he say, "Well, so I like to hear what kind o' spiel the young hoosier statesman from the banks o' the Wabash was gine 'em, anyhow."

An' Tookpafka Micco he go on an' say, "Well, so he tell 'em Oklahoma an' Injin Territory make a fine lookin' couple an' ought to had they picture taken together, so congress could have it enlarged an' hang it up on the map o' our common country. Then he go on an' warm up to the occasion an' pay a glowin' tribute to the pioneers. He say they was overcome the coyote an' exterminate the beaver an' chase all the deer out o' the country with hounds. They was replace the wild animals with domestic ones, like the thrifty razorback; they was chop down saplin's an' buil' huts; they was dig in the sod an' throw up rude abodes; they was laid the foundation o' a new state, an' give civilization a home in the backwoods. An' the woman folks was had a hand in it an' did most o' the work, the lord bless 'em! They was nurse the tow-headed kid with one arm an' made butter with the other one; they was brought in the wood an' cooked; they was make the garden an' slopped the pigs an' put something to eat on the table; they was picked the cotton an' pulled the corn an' made the children's clothes an' patched the old man's overalls; they was 'tended church on Sunday while the old man went to swap horses or' maybe so, set on the damp groun' in the bush playin' poker an' caught 'is death o' cold instead o' the winnin' hand. Then he go on an' tell 'em that was the kind o' people that make the new country fit to live in. He say they was all typical Americans an' Arkansawers, an' they was 'bout a million o' 'em ready for civilization. He say they all go to the new country with nothin' but a big start o' children. Some o' them was squatters an' boomers an' sooners an' intruders with a past, but they was want forgiveness now an' a chance to get back in the Union."

Then Hotgun he spit over the backlog an' say, "Well, so the young hoosier statesman from the banks o' the Wabash wasn't up on facts an' ancient hist'ry. He was just puttin' words together to see how many he had. The Injin was the only bona fide pioneer in this country, an' the Injin squaw was the woman that furnish the magic an' help overcome the wild animals an' carry civilization into the waste places with her sofky pestle an' mortar."

An' Tookpafka Micco he smoke slow and study long time an' say, "Well, so the Lord helps 'em that help 'emselves—except the Injin."

Letter of Fus Fixico, January 11, 1907

ALEXANDER POSEY

So it was Hotgun he had the woman folks make some sour bread an' some blue dumplings an' some hick'ry nut sofky an' some good sak ko-nip-kee* an' lots of ol' time dishes like that, for New Year. Then he was invite his frien's to come an' feast with him. Tokpafka Micco he was there, an' Wolf Warrior he was there, an' Kono Harjo he was there. They was all come soon an' bring their folks an' dogs an' staycd till put ncar sun down. Hotgun he was had a little white jug sittin' back under the bed to 'liven the conversation.

"Well, guess so," Tokpafka Micco he say, "Alfalfa Bill an' Boss Haskell† was put near ready to let their work so shine."

An' Hotgun he spit in the ashes an' say, "Well, so, not hardly. It was slow business to get started out right. It was take lots o' time to draw up the plans an' specifications. So, they didn't had none o' the immortal document written yet but the scare headlines, an' they was had a big confusion o' tongues before they get that far."

An' Tokpafka Micco he say, "Well so, what was the trouble anyhow?"

An' Hotgun he go on an' say, "Well, so, they couldn't decide, what name to give the Great Spirit, an' that bring up lots o' talk an' extra expense. Look like the Great Spirit was a stranger in the convention, an' none o' the delegates could remember His name. Boss

---

*Sofky and sak ko-nip-kee are traditional Creek dishes.

†Alfalfa Bill (William H. Murray) and Boss Haskell (Charles N. Haskell), along with Henry Asp, mentioned later, were three members of the conventions that called for statehood for Oklahoma. Murray, an intermarried Chickasaw citizen and tribal attorney, was the president of the Oklahoma Constitutional Convention. He got his name because he experimented with alfalfa. Haskell was a railroad promoter who became governor of Oklahoma. Asp, a prominent Republican, was the chief attorney for the Santa Fe Railroad in Oklahoma.

Haskell he think it was God, but no one was second his motion. An' Henry Asp he think it was the Supreme Ruler o' the Universe, but no one was agreed with him. An' Alfalfa Bill he say he believe it was Divine Providence, but there was no second to his motion neither. They was all three right, but they didn't know how to go ahead. So, while they was lockin' horns with one another, lot o' outsiders butt in with long petitions an' throw fat in the flames. There was a long petition from the unbelievers saying, 'Leave the Lord out.' An' there was another long petition from the pawn brokers sayin', 'Don't put Christ in it.' An' there was still another long petition from Zion City sayin' 'Dowie's the gen-u-wine article; beware of imitations.' Guess so, the petition about Misses Eddy was delayed."

Then Tokpafka Micco he smoke an' look under the bed an' say, "Well so, Alfalfa Bill an' Boss Haskell an' Henry Asp could settled their differences an' saved lots o' work for the printer an' give general satisfaction if they had recognized Confucius for the Chinaman, an' Bhudda for the Hindu, an' Mohamet for the Turk, an' Saint Patrick for the Irishman, an' the totem pole for the Eskimo, an' the almighty dollar for the American." (Wolf Warrior an' Kono Harjo give big grunt.)

An' Hotgun he say, "Well, so, otherwise the delegates was worked like one man an' head off lots o' future legislation for the new state. If a delegate was kicked over the trace chains an' tried to be insurgent Boss Haskell was named a few townships after him an' all was serene along the Potomac. Boss Haskell was a big medicine man an' had mighty influence. If he could make his men shovel dirt like he makes them vote ag'in their conscience, he could had the Panama canal dug maybe so in six weeks an' had time enough left to run for office on the independent ticket."

Then Tokpafka Micco he glanced his eye under the bed ag'in an' say, "Well, so, anyhow I druther kill time in the chimney corner an' spit over the backlog an' worry about what is goin' to become o' me than risk my political future in a one man pow-wow like that up to Guthrie."

*   *

John M. Oskison

*   *

John Milton Oskison was born on September 21, 1874, in Vinita in the Indian Territory. His mother, Rachel Critenden, was a quarter-blood Cherokee.

As a youth, Oskison attended Willie Halsell College together with Will Rogers. He received a bachelor's degree from Stanford University in 1889 and did some graduate work at Harvard in 1898–99 in the field of literature. His literary career began with the publication of a short story titled "I Match You, You Match Me" in the *Stanford Sequoia* in 1897.

In 1898 Oskison won *Century Magazine*'s annual short-story competition for college graduates with his story "Only the Master Shall Praise," and in 1904 he apparently received a "Black Cat" award for a story, titled "The Greater Appeal" (though a single reference to it is the only record of its existence). With some twenty short stories, many published by major American magazines, and three novels to his credit, he was undoubtedly one of the most successful of the early Indian writers of fiction.

From 1903 to 1906 Oskison was an exchange editor and editorial writer for the *New York Evening Post*, and from 1907 to 1910 he worked as a staff writer and associate editor for *Collier's Weekly*. He then became a writer on financial topics for various syndicated newspapers. Oskison also wrote quite extensively on Indian topics, including numerous articles for Indian-school journals and for the *Quarterly Journal of the Society of American Indians* (later the *American Indian Magazine*). He was an advocate of higher education and professional training for Indians. He served in World War I as a lieutenant in the army and then became a correspondent and relief distribution advisor for the American Expeditionary Forces in Europe in 1918 and 1919.

His publications include three novels: *Wild Harvest* (New York: D. Appleton and Co., 1925), *Black Jack Davy* (New York: D. Appleton and Co., 1926), and *Brothers Three* (New York: Macmillan Co., 1935); a biographical novel: *A Texas Titan: The Story of Sam Houston* (Garden City, N.Y.: Doubleday, Doran and Co., 1929); a history: *Tecumseh and His Times* (New York: G. P. Putnam's Sons, 1938); and many articles and short stories published between 1895 and 1925. Oskison died on February 25, 1947, in Tulsa, Oklahoma.

REFERENCES

Larson, Charles. *American Indian Fiction*. Albuquerque: University of New Mexico Press, 1978.
Oaks, Priscilla. "The First Generation of Native American Novelists." *MELUS* 5 (Spring 1978): 57–65. This and the Larson work discuss Oskison's novels together with those of other authors.
Strickland, Arney L. "John Milton Oskison: A Writer of the Transitional Period of the Oklahoma Indian Territory." *Southwestern American Literature* 2 (Winter 1972): 125–134.

STORIES BY JOHN M. OSKISON

"I Match You, You Match Me." *Indian Chieftain*, May 27, 1897, 1.
"Tookh Steh's Mistake." *Indian Chieftain*, July 22, 1897, 1–2.
"A Schoolmaster's Dissipation." *Indian Chieftain*, December 23, 1897, 3.
"Only the Master Shall Praise." *Century Magazine*, January 1900, 327–335.
"When the Grass Grew Long." *Century Magazine*, June 1901, 247–250.
"To Younger's Bend." *Frank Leslie's Monthly*, June 1903, 182–188.
"The Fall of King Chris." *Frank Leslie's Monthly*, October 1903, 586–593.
"The Quality of Mercy: A Story of the Indian Territory." *Century Magazine*, June 1904, 178–181.
"The Problem of Old Harjo." *Southern Workman*, April 1907, 235–241.
"Young Henry and the Old Man." *McClure's*, June 1908, 237–239.
"Koenig's Discovery." *Collier's*, May 28, 1910, 20–21, 31–32.
"Diverse Tongues: A Sketch." *Current Literature* 49 (September 1910): 343–344.
"Out of the Night that Covers." *Delineator* 78 (August 1911): 80, 125.

"Walla Tenaka-Creek." *Collier's*, July 12, 1913, 16–17.
"An Indian Animal Story." *Indian School Journal* 14 (January 1914): 213.
"Apples of the Hesperides, Kansas." *Forum* 51 (March 1914): 391–408.
"The Man Who Interfered." *Southern Workman*, October 1915, 557–563.
"The Other Partner." *Collier's*, December 6, 1924, 14–15, 30–32.
"The Singing Bird." *Sunset Magazine*, March 1925, 5–8.

The Problem of Old Harjo

JOHN M. OSKISON

The Spirit of the Lord had descended upon old Harjo. From the new missionary, just out from New York, he had learned that he was a sinner. The fire in the new missionary's eyes and her gracious appeal had convinced old Harjo that this was the time to repent and be saved. He was very much in earnest, and he assured Miss Evans that he wanted to be baptized and received into the church at once. Miss Evans was enthusiastic and went to Mrs. Rowell with the news. It was Mrs. Rowell who had said that it was no use to try to convert the older Indians, and she, after fifteen years of work in Indian Territory missions, should have known. Miss Evans was pardonably proud of her conquest.

"Old Harjo converted!" exclaimed Mrs. Rowell. "Dear Miss Evans, do you know that old Harjo has two wives?" To the older woman it was as if someone had said to her "Madame, the Sultan of Turkey wishes to teach one of your mission Sabbath school classes."

"But," protested the younger woman, "he is really sincere, and—

"Then ask him," Mrs. Rowell interrupted a bit sternly, "if he will put away one of his wives. Ask him, before he comes into the presence of the Lord, if he is willing to conform to the laws of the country in which he lives, the country that guarantees his idle existence. Miss Evans, your work is not even begun." No one who knew Mrs. Rowell would say that she lacked sincerity and patriotism. Her own cousin was an earnest crusader against Mormonism, and had gathered a goodly share of that wagonload of protests that the Senate had been asked to read when it was considering whether a certain statesman of Utah should be allowed to represent his state at Washington.

In her practical, tactful way, Mrs. Rowell had kept clear of such embarrassments. At first, she had written letters of indignant protest to the Indian Office against the toleration of bigamy amongst the tribes. A wise inspector had been sent to the mission, and this man had pointed out that it was better to ignore certain things, "deplorable, to be sure," than to attempt to make over the habits of the old men. Of course, the young Indians would not be permitted to take more than one wife each."

So Mrs. Rowell had discreetly limited her missionary efforts to the young, and had exercised toward the old and bigamous only that strict charity which even a hopeless sinner might claim.

Miss Evans, it was to be regretted, had only the vaguest notions about "expediency"; so weak on matters of doctrine was she that the news that Harjo was living with two wives didn't startle her. She was young and possessed of but one enthusiasm—that for saving souls.

"I suppose," she ventured, "that old Harjo *must* put away one wife before he can join the church?"

"There can be no question about it, Miss Evans."

"Then I shall have to ask him to do it." Miss Evans regretted the necessity for forcing this sacrifice, but had no doubt that the Indian would make it an order to accept the gift of salvation which she was commissioned to bear to him.

Harjo lived in a "double" log cabin three miles from the mission. His ten acres of corn had been gathered into its fence-rail crib; four hogs that were to furnish his winter's bacon had been brought in from the woods and penned conveniently near to the crib; out in a corner of the garden, a fat mound of dirt rose where the crop of turnips and potatoes had been buried against the corrupting frost; and in the hayloft of his log stable were stored many pumpkins, dried corn, onions (suspended in bunches from the rafters) and the varied forage that Mrs. Harjo number one and Mrs. Harjo number two had thriftily provided. Three cows, three young heifers, two colts, and two patient, capable mares bore the Harjo brand, a fantastic "**H‑I**" that the old man had designed. Materially, Harjo was solvent; and if the Government had ever come to his aid he could not recall the date.

This attempt to rehabilitate old Harjo morally, Miss Evans felt, was not one to be made at the mission; it should be undertaken in the Creek's own home, where the evidences of his sin should confront him as she explained.

When Miss Evans rode up to the block in front of Harjo's cabin, the old Indian came out, slowly and with a broadening smile of welcome on his face. A clean gray flannel shirt had taken the place of the white collarless garment, with crackling stiff bosom, that he had worn to the mission meetings. Comfortable, well-patched moccasins had been substituted for creaking boots, and brown corduroys, belted in at the waist, for tight black trousers. His abundant gray hair fell down on his shoulders. In his eyes, clear and large and black, glowed the light of true hospitality. Miss Evans thought of the patriarchs as she saw him lead her horse out to the stable; thus Abraham might have looked and lived.

"Harjo," began Miss Evans before following the old man to the covered passageway between the disconnected cabins, "is it true that you have two wives?" Her tone was neither stern nor accusatory. The Creek had heard that question before, from scandalized missionaries and perplexed registry clerks when he went to Muscogee to enroll himself and his family in one of the many "final" records ordered to be made by the Government preparatory to dividing the Creek lands among the individual citizens.

For answer, Harjo called, first into the cabin that was used as a kitchen and then, in a loud, clear voice, toward the small field, where Miss Evans saw a flock of half-grown turkeys running about in the corn stubble. From the kitchen emerged a tall, thin Indian woman of fifty-five, with a red handkerchief bound severly over her head. She spoke to Miss Evans and sat down in the passageway. Presently, a clear, sweet voice was heard in the field; a stout, handsome woman, about the same age as the other, climbed the rail fence and came up to the house. She, also, greeted Miss Evans briefly. Then she carried a tin basin to the well nearby, where she filled it to the brim. Setting it down on the horse block, she rolled back her sleeves, tucked in the collar of her gray blouse, and plunged her face in the water. In a minute she came out of the kitchen freshened and smiling. 'Liza Harjo had been pulling dried bean stalks at one end of the field, and it was dirty work. At last old Harjo turned to

Miss Evans and said, "These two my wife—this one 'Liza, this one Jennie."

It was done with simple dignity. Miss Evans bowed and stammered. Three pairs of eyes were turned upon her in patient, courteous inquiry.

It was hard to state the case. The old man was so evidently proud of his women, and so flattered by Miss Evans' interest in them, that he would find it hard to understand. Still, it had to be done, and Miss Evans took the plunge.

"Harjo, you want to come into our church?" The old man's face lighted.

"Oh, yes, I would come to Jesus, please, my friend."

"Do you know, Harjo, that the Lord commanded that one man should mate with but one woman?" The question was stated again in simpler terms, and the Indian replied, "Me know that now, my friend. Long time ago"—Harjo plainly meant the whole period previous to his conversion— "me did not know. The Lord Jesus did not speak to me in that time and so I was blind. I do what blind man do."

"Harjo, you must have only one wife when you come into our church. Can't you give up one of these women?" Miss Evans glanced at the two, sitting by with smiles of polite interest on their faces, understanding nothing. They had not shared Harjo's enthusiasm either for the white man's God or his language.

"Give up my wife?" A sly smile stole over his face. He leaned closer to Miss Evans. "You tell me, my friend, which one I give up." He glanced from 'Liza to Jennie as if to weigh their attractions, and the two rewarded him with their pleasantest smiles. "You tell me which one," he urged.

"Why, Harjo, how can I tell you!" Miss Evans had little sense of humor; she had taken the old man seriously.

"Then," Harjo sighed, continuing the comedy, for surely the missionary was jesting with him, " 'Liza and Jennie must say." He talked to the Indian women for a time, and they laughed heartily. 'Liza, pointing to the other, shook her head. At length Harjo explained, "My friend, they cannot say. Jennie, she would run a race to see which one stay, but 'Liza, she say no, she is fat and cannot run."

Miss Evans comprehended at last. She flushed angrily, and protested, "Harjo, you are making a mock of a sacred subject; I cannot allow you to talk like this."

"But did you not speak in fun, my friend?" Harjo queried, sobering. "Surely you have just said what your friend, the white woman at the mission (he meant Mrs. Rowell) would say, and you do not mean what you say."

"Yes, Harjo, I mean it. It is true that Mrs. Rowell raised the point first, but I agree with her. The church cannot be defiled by receiving a bigamist into its membership." Harjo saw that the young woman was serious, distressingly serious. He was silent for a long time, but at last he raised his head and spoke quietly, "It is not good to talk like that if it is not in fun."

He rose and went to the stable. As he led Miss Evans' horse up to the block it was champing a mouthful of corn, the last of a generous portion that Harjo had put before it. The Indian held the bridle and waited for Miss Evans to mount. She was embarrassed, humiliated, angry. It was absurd to be dismissed in this way by—"by an ignorant old bigamist!" Then the humor of it burst upon her, and its human aspect. In her anxiety concerning the spiritual welfare of the sinner Harjo, she had insulted the man Harjo. She began to understand why Mrs. Rowell had said that the old Indians were hopeless.

"Harjo," she begged, coming out of the passageway, "please forgive me. I do not want you to give up one of your wives. Just tell me why you took them."

"I will tell you that, my friend." The old Creek looped the reins over his arm and sat down on the block. "For thirty years Jennie has lived with me as my wife. She is of the Bear people, and she came to me when I was thirty-five and she was twenty-five. She could not come before, for her mother was old, very old, and Jennie, she stay with her and feed her.

"So, when I was thirty years old I took 'Liza for my woman. She is of the Crow people. She help me make this little farm here when there was no farm for many miles around.

"Well, five years 'Liza and me, we live here and work hard. But there was no child. Then the old mother of Jennie she died, and Jennie got no family left in this part of the country. So 'Liza say to me, 'Why don't you take Jennie in here?' I say, 'You don't care?' and she say, 'No, maybe we have children here then.' But we have no children—never have children. We do not like that, but God He would not let it be. So, we have lived here thirty years very happy. Only just now you make me sad."

"Harjo," cried Miss Evans, "forget what I said. Forget that you wanted to join the church." For a young mission worker with a single purpose always before her, Miss Evans was saying a strange thing. Yet she couldn't help saying it; all of her zeal seemed to have been dissipated by a simple statement of the old man.

"I cannot forget to love Jesus, and I want to be saved." Old Harjo spoke with solemn earnestness. The situation was distracting. On one side stood a convert eager for the protection of the church, asking only that he be allowed to fulfill the obligations of humanity and on the other stood the church, represented by Mrs. Rowell, that set an impossible condition on receiving old Harjo to itself. Miss Evans wanted to cry; prayer, she felt, would be entirely inadequate as a means of expression.

"Oh! Harjo," she cried out, "I don't know what to do. I must think it over and talk with Mrs. Rowell again."

But Mrs. Rowell could suggest no way out; Miss Evans' talk with her only gave the older woman another opportunity to preach the folly of wasting time on the old and "unreasonable" Indians. Certainly the church could not listen even to a hint of a compromise in this case. If Harjo wanted to be saved, there was one way and only one—unless—

"Is either of the two women old? I mean, so old that she is—an—"

"Not at all," answered Miss Evans. "They're both strong and—yes, happy. I think they will outlive Harjo."

"Can't you appeal to one of the women to go away? I dare say we could provide for her." Miss Evans, incongruously, remembered Jennie's jesting proposal to race for the right to stay with Harjo.

What could the mission provide as a substitute for the little home that 'Liza had helped to create there in the edge of the woods? What other home would satisfy Jennie?

"Mrs. Rowell, are you sure that we ought to try to take one of Harjo's women from him? I'm not sure that it would in the least advance morality amongst the tribe, but I'm certain that it would make three gentle people unhappy for the rest of their lives."

"You may be right, Miss Evans." Mrs. Rowell was not seeking to create unhappiness, for enough of it inevitably came to be pictured in the little mission building. "You may be right," she repeated, "but it is a grievous misfortune that old Harjo should wish to unite with the church."

No one was more regular in his attendance at the mission meetings than old Harjo. Sitting well forward, he was always in plain view of Miss Evans at the organ. Before the service began, and after it was over, the old man greeted the young woman. There was never a spoken question, but in the Creek's eyes was always a mute inquiry.

Once Miss Evans ventured to write to her old pastor in New York, and explain her trouble. This was what he wrote in reply: "I am surprised that you are troubled, for I should have expected you to rejoice, as I do, over this new and wonderful evidence of the Lord's reforming power. Though the church cannot receive the old man so long as he is confessedly a bigamist and violator of his country's just laws, you should be greatly strengthened in your work through bringing him to desire salvation."

"Oh! it's easy to talk when you're free from responsibility!" cried out Miss Evans. "But I woke him up to a desire for this water of salvation that he cannot take. I have seen Harjo's home, and I know how cruel and useless it would be to urge him to give up what he loves—for he does love those two women who have spent half their lives and more with him. What, what can be done?"

Month after month, as old Harjo continued to occupy his seat in the mission meetings, with that mute appeal in his eyes and a persistent light of hope on his face, Miss Evans repeated the question, "What can be done?" If she was sometimes tempted to say to the old man, "Stop worrying about your soul; you'll get to Heaven as surely as any of us," there was always Mrs. Rowell to remind her that she was not a Mormon missionary. She could not run away from her perplexity. If she should secure a transfer to another station, she felt that Harjo would give up coming to the meetings, and in his despair become a positive influence for evil amongst his people. Mrs. Rowell would not waste her energy on an obstinate old man. No, Harjo was her creation, her impossible convert, and throughout the years, until death—the great solvent which is not always a solvent —came to one of them, would continue to haunt her.

And meanwhile, what?

The Singing Bird

JOHN M. OSKISON

"Now we talk, me and these Kee-too-wah fellows. Old woman, go to bed!"

Thus Jim Blind-Wolfe dismissed his wife, Jennie, who was not old. With the fleetest glancing look he pushed her gently toward the back door of the firelit cabin, one huge outspread hand covering both of her erect shoulders.

Big Jim, old Spring Frog, Panther and The Miller made up this inner, unofficial council of the Kee-too-wah organization that had met at Jim's cabin. Self-charged with the duty of carrying out the ancient command to maintain amongst the Cherokees the full-blood inheritance of race purity and race ideals, they would discuss an alarming late growth of outlawry in the tribe, an increase in crime due to idleness, drink and certain disturbing white men who had established themselves in the hills. Paradoxically, as they talked and planned secret pressures here and there, they would pass a jug of honest moonshine—but they would drink from it discreetly, lightly, as full-blood gentlemen should!

"Jim," old Spring Frog opened, "I hear my friend say something about that fellow you hit that day at Tahlequah—"

Jim's sudden, loud guffaw interrupted the old man.

"Him!" and Jim's scornful rumble summed up the case of Lovely Daniel, a wild half-breed neighbor.

Smiling at the muffled sound of Jim's laugh, Jennie Blind-Wolfe drew a gay shawl over the thick black hair that made a shining crown for her cleanly modeled head and oval brown face and went across, under the brilliant September starlight, to the out cabin where she was to sleep. It was an inviting pine-log room, pleasantly odorous of drying vegetables and smoked side meat hung from rafters.

She stood for a minute on the solid adz-hewn step listening to the faint, unintelligible murmur of her husband's voice, the occasional comments of the others whom she had left crouched in front of glowing wood embers in the wide stone fireplace; to the music of Spavinaw creek racing over its rocky bed to Grand river; to the incessant, high-pitched chirring of crickets in the grass, the hysteric repetitions of katydids and the steady clamor of tree frogs yonder at the edge of the clearing.

A maddening sound, this all-night chorus of the little creatures of grass and forest! For ten nights, as she lay beside the relaxed bulk of her giant husband, she had strained her ears in the effort to hear above their din the sound of a horse's tramping at the timber edge and the sound of a man's footsteps coming across the dead grass of the clearing.

"Oh, why don't they stop! Why don't they stop!" she had cried, silently, in an agony of fear. But tonight—

No fear, no resentment of the chirring voices in the grass, the forest clatter; tonight she knew what was to happen. Tonight she would know the shivery terror, the illicit thrill of the singing bird, but she would not be afraid. Lovely Daniel had promised to come to her. Some time before dawn he would come to the edge of the clearing, repeat twice the call of the hoot-owl. He would come to the tiny window of the out cabin, and then—

Lovely had made a wonderful plan, a credit to his half-breed shrewdness, if not to his name! It had been born of his hatred of big Jim Blind-Wolfe and nourished by a growing fever of desire for Jennie. Enough of it he had revealed to Jennie to set her heart pounding, hang a fox-fire glow in her eyes.

She undressed in the streaming light of a moon just past the half and diamond bright stars that laid a brilliant oblong on the floor in front of the open door. Standing on a warm wolf rug beside the wide home-made bed, she stretched her lithe brown body. Then, comfortably relaxed, she recalled the beginning of Lovely's clever plan; a ripple of laughter, soft, enigmatic, rose to her lips.

The beginning dated from a torrid day of midsummer. The Cherokee tribal council was meeting in the box-like brick capitol, set among young oaks in a fenced square. In the shade, on the trampled grass of this capitol square, lounged a knot of councilmen, townsmen, gossips from the hill farms. Jim Blind-Wolfe—huge, smiling, dominating—was of the group, in which also stood Lovely Daniel. Alert, contentious, sharp of tongue, Lovely was sneering at the full-blood gospel that was being preached. Men grew restive under his jeers and mocking flings until at length Jim demanded the word. In slow, measured terms, as became a man of his impressive presence and bull-like voice, he summed up their drawn-out discussion:

"I tell you, Kee-too-wah fellows don't like this lease business. You lease your land to white man, and pretty soon you don't have any land; white man crowd you out! This here country is Eenyan (Indian) country, set aside for Eenyans. We want to keep it always for Eenyans. Such is belief of Kee-too-wahs, and I am Kee-too-wah!"

These were the words Jim repeated when he told Jennie of what followed. He described Lovely Daniel's quick, angry rush toward him, and mimicked his sharp retort:

"Kee-too-wah fellows—hell! They think they run this here country." Jim could not reproduce the sneer that twisted the half-breed's mouth as he went on: "Kee-too-wahs are fools. White man goin' to come anyway. Jim Blind-Wolfe—huh! Biggest dam' fool of all!" He ended with an evil gesture, the sure insult, and Jim's sledgehammer fist swung smoothly against the side of his head. Lovely's body, lifted by the blow, was flung sprawling. He lay motionless.

"Jim!" cried old Spring Frog, "maybe so you kill that fellow. Bouff!—My God, I don' like."

Jim carried Lovely Daniel across the road to the porch of the National House, while young Hunt ran for Doctor Beavertail. That grave half-breed came, rolled up his sleeves and set to work. His native skill, combined with his medical school knowledge, sufficed to bring Lovely back to consciousness by late afternoon.

Next morning, with the memory of Jim's devastating and widely advertised blow fresh in their minds, the councilmen—after much half jesting and half serious debate—passed a special Act and sent it to Chief Dennis for signature:

"*It shall be unlawful for Jim Blind-Wolfe to strike a man with his closed fist!*"

It was promptly signed and posted in the corridor of the capitol. Jim read it, and as he strode out into the square the thin line of his sparse mustache was lifted by a loud gust of laughter. Hailing the Chief, fifty yards away, he roared:

"Hey, Dennis, must I only slap that Lovely Daniel fellow next time?" The Chief met him at the centre of the square. In an undertone, he undertook a friendly warning:

"You want to watch out for that Daniel fellow, Jim. You mighty nigh killed him, and—I kind of wish you had! He's bad. Bad—" the Chief repeated soberly, and came closer to impress Jim by his words—"We aint got sure proof yet, but I'm satisfied it was Lovely Daniel that waylaid Blue Logan on the Fort Gibson road and killed him."

The Chief's low-toned confidences went on; and before he mounted the steps and went in to his battered old desk, he recalled:

"You have seen that Yellow Crest woman sometimes? She comes into town from the hills with stovewood and sits on her wagon, with a shawl always across her face. She was a pretty young woman six years ago, wife of Looney Squirrel. This Lovely Daniel took to hanging round, and Looney caught 'em—Yellow Crest and him. You are Kee-too-wah, Jim; you know what the old fellows do to a 'singing bird'?"

"Yes," Jim admitted, "they cut off the end of her nose!"

"Yes, they punish the woman so, and—" the Chief's face showed a shadow of passionate resentment— "they do nothing to the man! The old fellows, the Kee-too-wahs," he repeated, "still do that way. It was what Looney Squirrel did before he sent Yellow Crest from his cabin."

"Yes, I know," Jim assented.

"This Lovely Daniel is bad for women to know; a bad fellow for any woman to know, Jim!" The Chief eyed him shrewdly, pressed his piston-like arm in friendly emphasis before he walked slowly away.

On the long drive to his clearing beside Spavinaw creek, Jim weighed Chief Dennis' words. He thought of Jennie's fond care of Lovely Daniel's frail sister, Betsy, who was fighting a hopeless battle against tuberculosis in the cabin across the Spavinaw where she lived with Lovely.

"A bad fellow for any woman to know!" Jim repeated, with half closed, contemplative eyes as he urged his tough pony team along the stony road. He would have to think about that. He would have to take more notice of his wife, too—that gay, slender, laughing young woman who kept his cabin, clung adoringly to him, her eyes dancing, and flashed into song with the sudden, clear burst of a red-bird in early spring—

Lovely as a menace to himself was one thing, he considered; foolishly, he refused to believe that he might be in serious danger from the half-breed; he believed that Lovely was a boaster, a coward, and that he would be afraid of the prompt vengeance of Jim's friends. But Lovely as a menace to Jennie—well, no friend would serve him here, either to warn, fearing his wrath and the tiger-swipe of his great hand, or to avenge!

In direct fashion, Jim spoke to Jennie of his encounter with the half-breed, and repeated the Chief's words of warning. A passing gleam of fear rounded her eyes as she listened; it changed to a gay, defiant smile when her man added:

"I think you better not go to see Betsy anymore."

"No?" she queried, then very gravely: "she is awful low, Jim, and I am her friend." She sat studying her husband's face for many minutes, turned to the pots hanging in the fireplace with a tiny, secret smile. "I am Betsy's best friend," she reiterated coaxingly.

"Well," Jim conceded, stretching his great bulk negligently, "you watch out for that fellow, her brother!"

Some days later, Jennie rode to the capitol, sought Chief Dennis and asked:

"Is Jim in real danger from Lovely Daniel?"

"I think maybe he is in great danger, Jennie; but Jim does not agree with me on that!" The Chief's slow smile was a tribute to her husband's careless bravery.

"Ah, that would make it easier for Lovely," she said to herself softly.

Jennie's thoughts drifted back to various occasions when she had visited Betsy Daniel. Sometimes, but not often, as she sat with her friend or busied herself sweeping and airing the cabin, preparing a bowl of hominy, putting on a pot of greens and bacon, stripping husks from roasting ears, helping on a patchwork quilt, Lovely would come in. He would squat, a thin handsome figure, in front of the fire, sniff eagerly at the cooking pots, rise, move restlessly about. He would speak with Jennie of his hunting; he would talk of the white men he knew at Vinita, some of whom came to the Spavinaw hills in the late fall to chase deer with him and encourage him to become active in tribal politics. These men wished to spur him to active opposition to the reactionary full-bloods, the Kee-too-wahs, who bitterly resented white intrusion.

When Jennie was ready to leave, he would bring her pony to the door, hold his hand for her to step on as she mounted; and he would turn glittering black eyes and grinning face up to her as she gathered the reins to ride away. She had known of Yellow Crest's punishment; she knew that the full-bloods called the deceiving wife a "singing bird"; with notes to lure others than her mate; and in Lovely Daniel's eyes she had read an invitation to sing!

When Jim had thrashed the half-breed, she wondered if that invitation would still hold good. The end of her wondering and weighing was a resolve to find out.

Two weeks she waited and planned before riding across Spavinaw creek, and during that time news of Lovely Daniel drifted to her ears. He had crossed the line into Arkansas with one of the reckless Pigeon boys. They had secured whisky, had rioted in the streets of a border town, had been chased home to the hills by peace officers. The half-breed had brought back a new pistol from Maysville, and up and down the Illinois river and amongst his friends on Flint creek he had sprinkled ugly threats against Jim. In mid-August, when she knew that he was at home, Jennie rode across to Betsy.

For half an hour, as Jim Blind-Wolfe's wife made Betsy comfortable in a big chair beside the doorway and put the cabin to rights, Lovely sat on the doorstep digging at its worn surface with a pocket knife, saying nothing. Then he disappeared in the brush, to return presently with his saddle-horse. At sunset, after Jennie had cleared away the early supper dishes and tucked Betsy into bed, he was waiting to ride with her. Eyes lowered, fingers nervously caressing her pony's mane, Jennie rode in silence. They crossed Spavinaw at the lonely ford, where she had often seen deer come down to drink, and went slowly up the steep, pine-covered slope. Near Jim's clearing she stopped. Without raising her eyes, she put out her hand.

"Now you go back," she half whispered. "I see you again." Lovely crowded his horse close, took her hand, muttered:

"Look up, Jennie, let me see what is in your eyes!" But she turned her head away and answered:

"I am afraid of you, Lovely—good-by." She pressed his supple, eager fingers, urged her pony forward. He dared not pursue, and turned back; at the ford he whooped, uttering the primitive burst of sound that expressed for him hatred, lust, exultation. His wildcat eyes glowed. Back at his cabin, when he had loosed his hobbled horse to browse in the brush, he sat in the doorway conjuring up pictures of the evil he meant to do Jim Blind-Wolfe and his young and foolish wife. First, he would make Jennie a sinister, branded outcast in the sight of the tribe, and then after Jim had tasted that bitterness he would lay for him. There would be a shot. Someone would find him, a stiffening corpse, beside a lonely road! Until long after the new moon had sunk he sat, at times crooning fragments of old Cherokee songs, or flinging an occasional gay word to Betsy.

At Jennie's next visit, Betsy sent her brother to the Eucha settlement store for medicine. He had scarcely gone when Betsy called Jennie to her side, looking searchingly into her face.

"You are very dear to me, Jennie," she said in Cherokee, her hand stroking the other's face, fever-glowing eyes and a stain of tell-tale red on her thin cheeks emphasizing her anxiety. "Will you promise me that you will be wise, and careful—with Lovely? I do not want to lose you for the little time left to me!"

Jennie put her arm about her friend's wasted shoulders and leaned to whisper:

"My sister, you will not lose me."

"But Lovely—he is wild—he is Jim Blind-Wolfe's enemy—and I am afraid." Her words were hesitant, but suggestive.

"You are my friend," Jennie assured her quickly. "What I do will be best for both of us—and Lovely too! You will trust me?"

Betsy nodded, fell quiet under Jennie's gentle caresses.

Again Lovely rode across the ford with Jennie, rode close, begging for the promise that seemed to hang upon her lips; and before they parted she gave it, in a soft rush of speech:

"That will be hard, what you ask, Lovely, but some time when Jim is not with me I will let you know!" The half-breed's whoop at the ford punctuated a snatch of song.

Jennie was committed now. She quieted Jim's vague uneasiness at her visits to the cabin, by emphasizing Betsy's need of her care and asserting that Lovely's behavior was correct. By cunning degrees, she led the half-breed to reveal his plan for squaring accounts with her husband—that is, the part involving Jim's assassination. To Lovely's passionate outburst of hate she replied crooningly:

"Yes, I know. He hurt you, Lovely!"

By late August, when dying summer had released upon the night myriad insect sounds, above whose clamorous fiddling and chirring casual noises were hard to distinguish, she had stirred Lovely to a very frenzy of impatience. More than the desire of vengeance drew him now. He wanted Jennie for herself. He had sworn to come to her when the new moon was as wide, at the center of its crescent, as the red ribbon that bound her hair. He would come to the edge of the clearing some time before dawn—Jim would be asleep—and twice he would utter the hoot-owl's cry. She must slip out to him. If she did not, he swore that he would cross the clearing cat-footedly, open the door very slowly and quietly, come in and shoot Jim as he lay asleep. And then—

"Oh, no, not blood!" she cried, fighting desperately to alter his determination. He raved, boasted. She held out, pleading:

"No, no, not blood, in my sight! Wait until I come to you." As he persisted, she threatened: "If I hear you coming to the door, I will scream and Jim will rise up and kill you!"

Night after night she lay, sleeping fitfully, listening for the double owl cry, straining her ears to catch, above the high-pitched monotone of the insects' singing, the sound of footsteps in the dead grass. Twice during that time of waiting she visited Betsy and fought off Lovely's importunate advances with the warning:

"It must be safe—no blood. I will let you know."

The moon had filled its crescent, was swelling to fulness, before the opportunity Jennie had waited for arrived. Then Jim told her of the coming secret council in his cabin of the leaders of the Kee-too-wahs. They would eat supper and talk all night. She would prepare a pot of coffee for them, set it beside the fire and go to sleep in the out cabin. She weighed the peril, decided, and slipped across to Spavinaw to tell Lovely Daniel:

"Come to the out cabin before dawn, as you have said. Come to the little window that looks toward the creek. Tap, and I will open and say if all is safe." In a quick upward glance from her lowered eyes, Jennie saw the half-breed's grin of triumph. Trembling, she sent him back to the ford and his whooping rush up the opposite slope. In his eyes she had read—love of her? Yes; and death for Jim! Lovely's hatred of the giant who had all but killed him with a blow of his fist had become a crackling blaze in his breast.

Ten days of strain and nights of broken sleep had fined the edges of Jennie's nerves. She lay quite wide awake now, certain of herself, confident; and now she did not care about the foolish insect noises. She leaned out of bed to place her deerskin slippers at just the spot she desired to have them and hang a warm shawl over a chair where she could seize it with one movement of her hand. Fingers clasped behind her head, she lay watching a little square of starlit and moonlit sky through the window.

A rooster's crowing announced midnight; a little later she heard Jim's heavy step on the east porch of the main cabin as he emerged to sniff the fresh air, and then the slam of the door as he went in; she was aware of the pleasantly nipping coolness of the period before daybreak; again there was a stir on the east porch.

Cold, passionless men's business Jim and his three companions were busy about now. Impersonal, free from individual angers, jealousies, attachments, they sat, like remote, secret gods, in judgment on the conduct of a community, the policy of a tribe. Kee-too-wah tradition, the old conception of tribal integrity, the clean spirit of ancestors who had successfully fought against race deterioration and the decay of morale in the long years of contact with the whites in Georgia and Tennessee—these were their preoccupations. They harked back to legendary days, to the very beginning, when the Great Spirit had handed over to the tribe a sacred fire, with the injunction to keep it burning forever; and they strove to keep alive in the minds of an easy living, careless generation the memory of that road of Calvary over which their fathers and mothers had been driven when the then new Indian country was settled.

Jennie could understand but vaguely the purpose which dominated the four. It seemed shadowy, very different from the flaming, heart-stirring enterprise that concerned her! She lay taut-strung, like a bow made ready, thinking, feeling. Soon now, perhaps when the talk in the cabin had thinned and sleep was close to the eyelids of the four, she would hear a tapping at the window. She began to listen, to watch for a shadow at the little opening.

It came. Lovely's head and shoulders made a blur against the small luminous square; his tapping was as light as the flick of a bird's wing, insistent as the drumming of the male partridge in spring. Jennie stepped into her slippers, flung the shawl about her shoulders, flitted silently to the window.

She would not let him in at once. She knew the steps which she must take in order to test his ardor, stir him to impetuous frenzy. She knew the privilege of her who turned singing bird to savor the preliminary delights of song! She pushed the tiny sliding window aside a crack and whispered:

"Who has come?" At Lovely's fatuous answer, she laughed a faint ghost laugh and breathed: "Why have you come?" Then, before he could speak, "no, don't tell me; wait and let me talk with you here for a time."

In throaty whispers, only half coherent, the man pressed his suit.

Jennie went silent in the midst of his jumbled speeches, so stirred by inner turmoil that she scarcely heard his pleading. Then her trembling voice insisted:

"You must wait a little while longer, Lovely. I am afraid. But I will let you come in before it is light. I promise!" Her shawl was drawn across her face, and as she put timid fingers in his reaching hand he felt them shake. Again, in maddening repetition, she sang the refrain:

"Wait; and tell me once more what it is that you and I will do after tonight. Wait a little. I will not be afraid to let you in after a time." When he threatened to leave the window and go round to the door, she protested in great agitation:

"No, no. The bar is up against you, and if you rattle the door Jim will hear. He will come and spoil everything. He would—" her voice all but faded in her throat— "he would kill you, Lovely!"

At length the last note of the singing bird had been sounded, and Jennie answered to Lovely's frantic entreaty:

"Come now to the door swiftly and silently, in bare feet. Leave your coat there." She pointed, and stood breathless, watching his movements. He dropped shoes, coat, belt and pistol holster in a heap. With a gasp of relief, she ran to unbar the door.

"Quick!" she urged, pulling him into the blinding darkness. Then, close to his ear, "wait for me here!" She flashed by him, stepped through the doorway, closed him in and reached up to trip the stout greased bar that she had prepared. It slid noiselessly across to engage iron stirrups fixed in the heavy door and the massive logs of the door frame. Clasping her shawl tightly about her body, she ran to the cabin where Jim and his three friends sat in silence, cross-legged in front of the fireplace. She opened the door and called:

"Jim!" He jerked his head up, rose. "Don't be troubled," she told the others. "Jim will be back soon." She shut the door as the great bulk of her husband emerged.

"Quick, Jim, come with me." She seized his big paw and dragged at it. "Quick! quick!" He followed at a lumbering trot, dazed and uttering fragments of questions. To the back of the out cabin she led him, ran to the dark heap of Lovely Daniel's clothes, seized belt, holster and pistol and thrust them into Jim's hands.

"Here, what's this!" he bellowed. Inside there was the sound of bare feet rushing across the floor, an ineffectual yank at the door, a snarl of disappointed rage—then silence.

"Jim!" His wife was on tiptoe in the effort to bring her lips nearer to his ear.

"In there is Lovely Daniel. He came to kill you, Jim—Listen, Jim: he came to kill you, do you understand? I knew why he was coming and I—I made him believe I was a—a singing bird, Jim! And he came to me first—. But I did not, Jim—I put down the outside bar that I had fixed, as soon as he came in, and ran to you—. Come and see. Come and see how I fixed it." She pulled him round to the door, showed him the bar firm in its place. "See, I fixed it so to trap him. You see, Jim?"

A faint glimmer of daylight had come, and big Jim stooped to look into the shining eyes of his wife. His gaze was like a down-thrust knife, cutting clean and deep into her soul. It found there only a turbulent fear for him, a sunburst of adoration that excited in him a surge of primitive joy. He came erect.

"Ah, you Lovely Daniel!" he shouted savagely. "You try to make singing bird out of my wife!" He broke into the old Cherokee killer's dread warning, the wild turkey's gobble.

With his hand on the door, and before he could lift the bar, he saw his friends emerge from the main cabin. Old Spring Frog peered round the corner from the east porch. He had heard the turkey gobbler signal! Jim thought swiftly; these men must not know that Lovely Daniel was in the out cabin, where his wife had slept. In a voice forced to calmness, he called to Spring Frog:

"I just now hear a big old gobbler, yonder." He pointed across the clearing toward the creek. The three returned to their places in front of the fire.

Jim flung up the outer bar, swung the door wide and struck aside the knife-armed hand that leaped toward his breast. The weapon dropped, and Jim grabbed Lovely by the shirt to drag him forth.

"Put on your clothes," he ordered. With one hand helpless from the force of Jim's blow, the half-breed made slow progress with his dressing, and Jim had time to think, to make a little plan of his own. With shawl drawn closely about her body and over her head, Jennie stood waiting at the corner of the out cabin, watching the dawn change from gray to pink-shot silver.

Dressed, Lovely Daniel stood still, in a sort of frozen apathy, awaiting he wondered what terrible retribution. Jim grasped his arm, turned his head to speak to Jennie:

"Stay in here until I come." She disappeared into the shadowy cabin, closed the door, ran to crouch against the thick pillow and the rude headboard of the bed—and waited.

Jim led the half-breed round to the east porch of the main cabin, opened the door and thrust him into view of his friends. They looked up, curious, expectant.

"Ah," muttered old Spring Frog, "I did hear what I heard!"— Jim's warning gobble.

"This fellow—" Jim shoved Lovely Daniel close to the cross-legged group— "come to kill me. My wife, she hear him coming and she run to tell me just now." He fell silent, waited for a minute, then:

"You know this fellow, what I done to him. You know this fellow, how he kill Blue Logan, how he make Yellow Crest outcast woman, how he make Looney Squirrel a man ashamed—We get rid of this fellow?" The last words were more a statement than a question, but his friends nodded assent.

"Let that be done," Old Spring Frog, staunch Kee-too-wah defender of Indian probity, made a sign; it was repeated by Panther and The Miller. The three rose to stand beside Jim Blind-Wolfe.

Sure of his friends now, Jim's face framed a smile, a kind of savage radiance. He spoke rapidly for a minute, reached for the brown whisky jug that was a blob of darkness on the wide, lighted hearth —the jug from which the four had drunk sparingly throughout the night. Still smiling, he handed it to the half-breed.

"This fellow like whisky—drink!" Lovely Daniel took the jug, tilted it and drank deep, the Adam's apple in his lean throat working rhythmically as he gulped the raw, hot liquor. When at last he removed the jug from his lips he shook it to show how little remained.

They would not say that he had been afraid to drink! Jim's smile turned to a low laugh as he spoke to his friends:

"I take this fellow outside now; you wait here for me few minutes."

The two stepped out to the east porch, facing a fast-mounting radiance that presaged the coming of sunrise. Jim carried the half-breed's pistol. He led Lovely Daniel to the end of the porch; they stood in silence, Jim's eyes fixed on the other's face. At the edge of the clearing they heard a crow's awakening "caw! caw!" and the jarring call of a jaybird.

Jim spoke musingly, earnestly:

"Listen, Lovely Daniel: If you want to do that, you can go away from here—clear away from all Cherokee people, and I will not kill you!" Jim's stunning speech hung suspended, and Lovely's eyes sought his face; he resumed: "If you go away, it must be for all time. You must be outcast always. You try to come back, Kee-too-wah will know and I will then kill you. You know that?" The other nodded somberly. Jim spoke again, his gaze boring into eyes that wavered: "But I don't think you want to go away, like that, to stay always, lost man. Well, then?

"Listen: I will tell you one other way. Like this, Lovely Daniel —you can go up yonder, if you are brave man—" solemnly Jim pointed to the crimson-streaked sky— "on the back of the sun! Old Cherokee folks tell about how Eenyans go home to Great Spirit on the back of the sun. I don't know; maybe so; you can try—You try?" His face had become stern now, and menacing; he bent close to peer into the drink-flushed face of the half-breed.

Lovely Daniel weighed the alternatives swiftly. Reeling, aflame with the fiery liquid he had drunk, his mind seized upon Jim's suggestion.

"I go with the sun!" he cried, swaying toward the edge of the porch. Boastfully, exultantly, he demanded, "Give me my gun." Jim handed him the pistol, stepped backwards noiselessly, his eyes holding Lovely. His hand on the latch, he stopped.

Lovely Daniel's uninjured hand, loosely gripping the pistol, hung at his side as he watched the full daylight spread down to the edge of the clearing. Out of some deep, long-hidden spring of memory rose a fragment of wild song, a chant of death. It mounted to a fervid burst, as the sharp red edge of the sun appeared; it ended in a triumphant whoop—and the roar of the pistol, pressed against his temple, sent a perching crow whirling upwards with a startled "caw!"

Jim stepped inside.

"What was that?" Spring Frog questioned perfunctorily.

"Lovely Daniel was making answer," Jim responded enigmatically.

"Making answer? To what?"

"Oh, a singing bird, I think—early morning singing bird, I think." He looked into the faces of his friends until he knew that they understood, then turned to go out. He lingered to say:

"If you fellows go look out for that which was Lovely Daniel, I get my wife to come and cook breakfast for us."

He found Jennie still crouched on the bed, hands still clapped tight against her ears. He gathered her into his arms, a vast tenderness and a fierce pride in her courage thrilling through him. With her face buried beneath his cheek and her arms tight about his neck, he sat on the bed and whispered:

"All is well now, all is well!" Her convulsive hold on him tightened.

"Oh, my Jim!" she breathed fiercely and, after a minute, "I can go now and care for Betsy without fear."

"Yes." Jim's eyes sought the brilliant oblong of daylight that was the doorway, and his voice was tender and solemn as he added:

"You can go to Betsy now, and tell her that Lovely went home without fear, on the back of the sun. I think she will understand what you say—Pretty soon you come and cook breakfast?"

"Pretty soon, I come," she echoed and, shivering, settled even closer to the great bulk of her husband.

John Joseph Mathews

John Joseph Mathews was born on November 16, 1894, at the Osage agency in Pawhuska in the Indian Territory. His father, William Shirley Mathews, was a quarter-blood Osage, and his mother was of French ancestry. He was listed on the 1906 tribal roll as being one-eighth Osage.

John Mathews received his basic education at Mrs. Tucker's Subscription School, the St. Joseph Parochial School, and Pawhuska High School. In 1914 he began to study geology at the University of Oklahoma, but he had to interrupt his studies for three years to serve in the army during World War I, first in the cavalry and then as an aviator in the Signal Corps. After his graduation from the University of Oklahoma in 1920, he enrolled at Oxford University and received a B.A. Oxon in natural science three years later. Mathews then attended the University of Geneva's School for International Relations, completing a program for an international relations certificate in 1924. During his sojourn in Geneva, he worked part-time as a League of Nations correspondent for the *Philadelphia Ledger*. Following this, he spent several years traveling around Europe and Africa; apparently his share of Osage oil dividends made him financially independent. At one point in the course of his travels, he began to reconsider his Osage heritage and, after having spent some time in Los Angeles as a real estate broker, decided to return to Pawhuska permanently in 1929.

Mathews's literary career began with a series of adventure sketches published in *Sooner Magazine*, the alumni journal of the University of Oklahoma, between 1929 and 1933. These dealt primarily with his own experiences as a big-game hunter. In 1932 he published *Wah'Kon Tah: The Osage and the White Man's Road* (reprint, Norman: University of Oklahoma Press, 1968), an account of Osage life based on the journals of agent Laban J. Miles. This publication was selected by the Book of the Month Club, which encouraged him to continue his studies of Osage history.

At the same time, Mathews became involved in Osage tribal affairs. In 1934 he was elected to the Osage Council, serving two consecutive four-year terms. He was also instrumental in the establishment of the Osage Tribal Museum in 1938 and its consequent funding. He supported John Collier's administration of the BIA and favored Osage acceptance of the Indian Reorganization Act of 1934.

In 1934 Mathews published *Sundown* (N.Y.: Longmans, Green and Co.; reprint, Norman: University of Oklahoma Press, 1988), a semiautobiographical novel about an Osage youth experiencing the problem of cultural marginality. His next book, *Talking to the Moon* (Chicago: University of Chicago Press; reprint, Norman: University of Oklahoma Press, 1981), appeared in 1945. It is an account of his voluntary seclusion at a remote ranch and is basically a lengthy contemplation on man and nature somewhat reminiscent of *Walden*. Altogether different is his *Life and Death of an Oilman: The Career of E. W. Marland* (Norman: University of Oklahoma Press, 1951), the biography of his friend, Governor Ernest Marland. Mathews's major work, on which he is said to have spent some thirty years, is *The Osages: Children of the Middle Waters* (Norman: University of Oklahoma Press, 1961; reprint, 1981). Its nearly eight hundred pages are based on oral-history interviews he conducted with tribal elders, a fact that has earned him both praise and criticism from historians concerning the book's authenticity. It begins with Osage accounts of creation and ends with the death of the noted Chief Lookout in 1949. Lastly, Mathews apparently completed a two-volume autobiography titled "Twenty Thousand Mornings," which was never published. He died on June 11, 1979.

REFERENCES

Bailey, Garrick. "John Joseph Mathews." In Margot Liberty, ed., *American Indian Intellectuals*, 205–214. Proceedings of the American Ethnological Society, 1976. St. Paul: West Publishing Company, 1978.

Hunter, Carol. "The Protagonist as Mixed-Blood in John Joseph Mathews' Novel: *Sundown.*" *American Indian Quarterly* 6 (Fall–Winter 1982): 319–337.

———. "The Historical Content in John Joseph Mathews' *Sundown.*" *MELUS* 9 (Spring 1982): 61–72.

Logsdon, G. "John Joseph Mathews: A Conversation." *Nimrod* 16 (April 1972): 70–75.

Wilson, Terry P. "Osage Oxonian: The Heritage of John Joseph Mathews." *Chronicles of Oklahoma* 59 (Fall 1981): 264–293.

STORIES BY JOHN JOSEPH MATHEWS

"The Trapper's Dog." *Sooner Magazine*, January 1931, 133, 141.
"Beauty's Votary." *Sooner Magazine*, February 1931, 171, 181–182.
"Ee Sa Rah N'cah's Story." *Sooner Magazine*, June 1931, 328–329.
"Ole Bob." *Sooner Magazine*, April 1933, 206–207.

Ee Sa Rah N'eah's Story

JOHN JOSEPH MATHEWS

Ee sa rah n'eah's hands were copper colored, long and graceful, and his feet in his buckskin moccasins seemed too small to bear his tall body; they were almost ludicrously small. The black roach topping his shaven head seemed to compensate for the board-flattened rear of his skull, and add inches to his great height. Many small wrinkles converged to the outside corners of his black, rather cruel, understanding eyes. But they always sparkled when Ee sa rah n'eah told a story.

When the women were decorating their men for the June dances, he could always be found on the edge of the camp, sitting cross-legged, in utter detachment, and there I always searched for him. Though I loved the kettle-drum and its circle of singers, and of course was fascinated by the gyrations of the gorgeous dancers, I grew weary of this spectacle through long familiarity. Of course a boy couldn't be expected to spend the whole of a delightful June day listening to endless harangue and experience an interest which only a full appreciation could create and maintain. Especially since Ee sa rah n'eah told stories, and at this time one was happiest in the realm of fantasy. Of course Ee sa rah n'eah had been a great hunter.

One morning we were seated on the grass at the edge of the camp. At times the sound of the drums was carried to us in full volume, then it died to distant thumping. At times the wind carried the singers' voices to us and then carried them away. But neither of us really heard the singers or the drums. Ee sa rah n'eah sat singing softly to himself, beating time with his fingers. "He-ooooh, ho-ooooh, ho-ooooh, ho-ooooh, ho-ooooh," he sang. Suddenly he stopped and pointed to where my sorrel mare was dragging her reins as she grazed. "Tompa," he said, "that horse peesha."

"No," I said, "she's a good horse."

"Ho, he's peesha."

"She can run faster'n an Indian pony."

"Ho, ho."

"Looks like you'd tell me why you think she's bad, then."

"Ho," his eyes almost danced, "he can't climb tree, aint it."

He laughed heartily and enjoyed my embarrassment. Then he became serious and sat for some minutes. Suddenly his face cracked into wrinkles again, and he pointed to the .22-calibre rifle hanging on my saddle; "you shoot little birds." Of course I couldn't tell him that I had just come from a buffalo hunt on the hills north of Soldier creek. I couldn't tell him that with the aid of jack-rabbits, a flexible imagination, and a wise old mare, who patronized with tired tolerance my crazy whims, that I had a most successful hunt. I said evasively: "Some day I'm gonna kill a panther."

"Sure, someday you kill a panther; maybe panther he go away then."

"Poppa's gonna take me deer huntin' too—when I get bigger."

"Lo-o-o-ong time ago we kill panther; your poppa, he kill 'em too."

"How does a panther go?"

He looked at me steadily for some time, then pointed north; "you know creek up there." I knew the creeks in the north part of the reservation, but I wanted to be sure that I could name the one he referred to, so I hesitated. He then took a stick and drew the drainage system of the northern region. He followed one of the streams with his finger, then placed a small pebble on a spot about three-fourths of the way up the stream.

"One time lo-o-o-ong time ago we go find deer here. Me and young Pawnee. He was young man, this Pawnee; just start to pull hair from his face. I didn't know if it would be good to find deer with this Pawnee. I didn't know if he was good man. They said he eat weed and go crazy. They said he kill his mother when he eat this weed, and he run away from his uncles, so he would live. They said he was no Pawnee; they said he come from lo-o-o-ong way, but he said he was Pawnee. I say I am not afraid of this young man; I say well, I go.

"We sleep one time then we find place. I said, 'well, there are lots of sign here; we will find deer here,' I said. When we come to canyon it is late; the sun is not purty high. I said to young Pawnee 'lagony,' I said. 'You wait here,' I said, 'I go to head of canyon; I wait for deer, then you go up canyon,' I said. 'If they smell you, they come by me,' I said. 'Lagony.'

"I go on south edge of canyon. Wind come from north. Deer can smell purty good. When I get to head of canyon, I hide and wait. Everything is purty still. Seem like everything sleep. Lo-o-o-ong time I wait. A squirrel come down a tree and look at me and I say he look funny and do like white man, tryin' to see ever thing and don't know nothin.' Purty soon he make noise—barkin' like white man talkin', cause he don't know what I am, and I say he's foolish.

"I hear sounds. Sometime a leaf fall in the canyon, but I know it ain't no deer. A little bird go up and down a tree makin' a little noise, and I know it ain't no deer neither. Purty soon the sun he goes down lower, and I say where is this Pawnee; gu-whiz I say, he sure is slow, this Pawnee. Many thoughts come to my head; I think about what my wife say three days ago. I think what kind of man is the new agent; I say maybe he is good to Indian. Lo-o-o-ong time I sit like this with many thought in my head, but the Pawnee, he don't come. I say it sure is gettin' cold. I look and the sun, he is nearly down; I watch him change. He make yellow and pink and then he makes red. I say he sure is raisin' hell in the west, and I say it sure is purty. But I say that Pawnee sure is slow.

"Purty soon the Pawnee shoots, and I hear him down in the canyon when he shoots. I hear a funny noise too; I say I don't know what it is. I say it ain't no woman screamin' like someone stick a knife in him. It sure sound like that; like someone stickin' a knife in a woman. I say it can't be a woman dyin'; there ain't no woman here I say. Everything seem like it's 'fraid. Everthing's quiet like everthing's 'fraid of woman screamin'. The squirrel he quit barkin' and he think I don't see him flat on a limb. But I know it ain't no woman screamin' and I say I go down in the canyon and see.

"Purty soon I see this Pawnee, and I say he is dead, this Pawnee. He is on his face, and his gun is in his hand, and I say sure he is dead. Lo-o-o-ong time I stand and look at the cliff. I look up the canyon and down the canyon, and I can't see nothin'. I walk around this Pawnee; many times I walk round him, until I'm far away from him, and I say I see no sign; this is funny I say. Purty soon I look back and see this Pawnee move. I go over to him and he sit up and look at me. I said 'what sound like a woman screamin'.' He look at me scared, and then he look foolish. He said: 'panther he stand on that cliff and I shoot at him and he jump on me and knock me down.'

" 'You do not shoot good,' I said.

" 'Yes,' he said, 'I shoot good.'

" 'No, I believe you do not shoot good,' I said.

" 'This panther has in him the evil spirit,' he said.

" 'Ho, a panther can't carry the evil spirit,' I said.

" 'Yes,' he said, 'it is the evil spirit.'

"I go down to the cliff where the panther was and I look good. Purty soon I see the panther at the foot of the cliff, and I say he is dead. I go there and he is dead. I see that he is shot in the heart, and I say the Pawnee is weak and he faint. This Pawnee faint when the panther scream like a woman killed with a knife, I say."

D'Arcy McNickle

William D'Arcy McNickle was born on January 18, 1904, in St. Ignatius, Montana, on the Flathead Indian Reservation. His mother, Philomene Paranteau, was an adopted Flathead of Creek descent. He was registered as a quarter-blood member of the Confederated Salish and Kutenai Tribes.

In 1913 the superintendant of the reservation sent him to the Chemewa Indian Boarding School in Oregon, where he remained for a period of three years. Upon his return he attended public schools in Montana and Washington. Following his mother's divorce, McNickle took the name of Dahlberg (from his stepfather's name), but in 1933, at the birth of his first daughter, he resumed his original family name. Some of his earliest publications therefore appeared under the name D'Arcy Dahlberg.

McNickle studied at the University of Montana from 1921 to 1925, and his first short stories were published in the university's literary journal, *Frontier and Midland*. In 1925 he sold his allotment on the Flathead Reservation in order to study at Oxford. Three years later he settled in New York City to work as a free-lance writer. He remained in New York until 1936, interrupting his sojourn briefly in 1931 to enroll in a summer program at the University of Grenoble in France. He also attended courses at Columbia University in 1933.

In New York he completed his first novel, *The Surrounded* (New York: Dodd, Mead, 1936; reprint, Albuquerque: University of New Mexico Press, 1978). The year of its publication he left for Washington to join the Federal Writers' Project. In 1936 he also joined John Collier's staff in the BIA, serving consecutively as a field representative, assistant to the commissioner, and director of tribal relations until 1952. At this time he chose to quit the BIA because of its shift toward a policy of terminating federal services to Indians (House Concurrent Resolution 108) and instead to direct American Indian Development, Inc., at Boulder, Colorado. McNickle was also one of the cofounders of the National Congress of American Indians in 1944.

In 1949 McNickle published his first history, *They Came Here First* (New York: Lippincott; rev. ed., New York: Harper & Row, 1975). He then became increasingly involved in academic life, acting as a visiting lecturer at Regis College in Denver beginning in 1954. In 1966 he was appointed chairman of the newly established Department of Anthropology at the University of Saskatchewan's Regina campus, where he remained until his retirement in 1971, after which he lived in Albuquerque.

McNickle was a prolific writer. In 1954 he published *Runner in the Sun* (New York: Winston; reprint, Albuquerque: University of New Mexico Press, 1987), a juvenile novel with a Pueblo setting, and followed this in 1959 with *Indians and Other Americans* (New York: Harper & Row), a study of Indian affairs written in cooperation with Harold E. Fey. The Oxford University Press brought out his *Indian Tribes of the United States*, an ethnohistory, in 1962 (it was revised and updated as *Native American Tribalism* in 1973). He was awarded a Guggenheim Fellowship for 1963–64, which allowed him to complete his biography of Oliver La Farge, titled *Indian Man* (Bloomington: Indiana University Press, 1971).

During his retirement he was appointed program director for the Center for the History of the American Indian at the Newberry Library in Chicago and, later, chairman of the center's advisory council. Today the center bears his name.

McNickle died on October 18, 1977, in Albuquerque. His novel *Wind from an Enemy Sky* (New York: Harper & Row, 1978; reprint, Albuquerque: University of New Mexico Press, 1988), was published posthumously and is considered by many to be one of the best Indian novels. During the 1920s and 1930s he also wrote a number of short stories, most of which were never published.

REFERENCES

Ortiz, Alfonso. "D'Arcy McNickle (1904–1977): Across the River and Up the Hill." *American Indian Journal* (April 1978): 12–16.
Owens, Louis. "The 'Map of the Mind': D'Arcy McNickle and the American Indian Novel." *Western American Literature* 19 (Winter 1985): 275–283.
Ruppert, James. *D'Arcy McNickle*. Boise State University Western Writers Series. Boise, Idaho: Boise State University, 1988.

STORIES BY D'ARCY MCNICKLE

"The Silver Locket." *Frontier*, 4 November 1923, 18–21.
"Clod the Magician." *Frontier*, 4 May 1924, 8–10.
"Going to School." *Frontier*, 9(4), May 1929: 339–346.
"Meat for God." *Esquire*, September 1935, 86, 120, 122.
"Train Time." *Indians at Work* 3 (March 15, 1936): 45–47.
"Snowfall." *Common Ground* 4 (Summer 1944): 75–82.

McNickle's unpublished stories, including "Hard Riding," were collected in Birgit Hans, ed., "The Hawk Is Hungry: An Annotated Anthology of D'Arcy McNickle's Short Fiction" (M.A. thesis, University of Arizona, 1986).

Train Time

D'ARCY MCNICKLE

On the depot platform everybody stood waiting, listening. The train has just whistled, somebody said. They stood listening and gazing eastward, where railroad tracks and creek emerged together from a tree-choked canyon.

Twenty-five boys, five girls, Major Miles—all stood waiting and gazing eastward. Was it true that the train had whistled?

"That was no train!" a boy's voice explained.

"It was a steer bellowing."

"It was the train!"

Girls crowded backward against the station building, heads hanging, tears starting; boys pushed forward to the edge of the platform. An older boy with a voice already turning heavy stepped off the weather shredded boardwalk and stood wide-legged in the middle of the track. He was the doubter. He had heard no train.

Major Miles boomed, "You! What's your name? Get back here! Want to get killed! All of you, stand back!"

The Major strode about, soldier-like, and waved commands. He was exasperated. He was tired. A man driving cattle through timber had it easy, he was thinking. An animal trainer had no idea of trouble. Let anyone try corraling twenty-thirty Indian kids, dragging them out of hiding places, getting them away from relatives and together in one place, then holding them, without tying them, until train time! Even now, at the last moment, when his worries were almost over, they were trying to get themselves killed!

Major Miles was a man of conscience. Whatever he did, he did earnestly. On this hot end-of-summer day he perspired and frowned and wore his soldier bearing. He removed his hat from his wet brow and thoughtfully passed his hand from the hair line backward. Words tumbled about in his mind. Somehow, he realized, he had to

162

vivify the moment. These children were about to go out from the Reservation and get a new start. Life would change. They ought to realize it, somehow—

"Boys—and girls—" there were five girls he remembered. He had got them all lined up against the building, safely away from the edge of the platform. The air was stifling with end-of-summer heat. It was time to say something, never mind the heat. Yes, he would have to make the moment real. He stood soldier-like and thought that.

"Boys and girls—" The train whistled, dully, but unmistakably. Then it repeated more clearly. The rails came to life, something was running through them and making them sing.

Just then the Major's eye fell upon little Eneas and his sure voice faltered. He knew about little Eneas. Most of the boys and girls were mere names; he had seen them around the Agency with their parents, or had caught sight of them scurrying behind tepees and barns when he visited their homes. But little Eneas he knew. With him before his eyes, he paused.

He remembered so clearly the winter day, six months ago, when he first saw Eneas. It was the boy's grandfather, Michel Lamartine, he had gone to see. Michel had contracted to cut wood for the Agency but had not started work. The Major had gone to discover why not.

It was the coldest day of the winter, late in February, and the cabin sheltered as it was among the pine and cottonwood of a creek bottom, was shot through by frosty drafts. There was wood all about them. Lamartine was a woodcutter besides, yet there was no wood in the house. The fire in the flat-topped cast-iron stove burned weakly. The reason was apparent. The Major had but to look at the bed where Lamartine lay, twisted and shrunken by rheumatism. Only his black eyes burned with life. He tried to wave a hand as the Major entered.

"You see how I am!" the gesture indicated. Then a nerve-strung voice faltered. "We have it bad here. My old woman, she's not much good."

Clearly she wasn't, not for wood-chopping. She sat close by the fire, trying with good natured grin to lift her ponderous body from a low seated rocking chair. The Major had to motion her back to her ease. She breathed with asthmatic roar. Wood-chopping was not within her range. With only a squaw's hatchet to work with, she could scarcely have come within striking distance of a stick of wood. Two blows, if she had struck them, might have put a stop to her laboring heart.

"You see how it is," Lamartine's eyes flashed.

The Major saw clearly. Sitting there in the frosty cabin, he pondered their plight and at the same time wondered if he would get away without coming down with pneumonia. A stream of wind seemed to be hitting him in the back of the neck. Of course, there was nothing to do. One saw too many such situations. If one undertook to provide sustenance out of one's own pocket there would be no end to the demands. Government salaries were small, resources were limited. He could do no more than shake his head sadly, offer some vague hope, some small sympathy. He would have to get away at once.

Then a hand fumbled at the door; it opened. After a moment's struggle, little Eneas appeared, staggering under a full armload of pine limbs hacked into short lengths. The boy was no taller than an ax handle, his nose was running, and he had a croupy cough. He dropped the wood into the empty box near the old woman's chair, then straightened himself.

A soft chuckling came from the bed. Lamartine was full of pride. "A good boy, that. He keeps the old folks warm."

Something about the boy made the Major forget his determination to depart. Perhaps it was his wordlessness, his uncomplaining wordlessness. Or possibly it was his loyalty to the old people. Something drew his eyes to the boy and set him to thinking. Eneas was handing sticks of wood to the old woman and she was feeding them into the stove. When the fire box was full a good part of the boy's armload was gone. He would have to cut more, and more, to keep the old people warm.

The Major heard himself saying suddenly: "Sonny, show me your woodpile. Let's cut a lot of wood for the old folks."

It happened just like that, inexplicably. He went even farther. Not only did he cut enough wood to last through several days, but when he had finished he put the boy in the Agency car and drove him to town, five miles there and back. Against his own principles, he bought a week's store of groceries, and excused himself by telling the boy, as they drove homeward, "Your grandfather won't be able to get to town for a few days yet. Tell him to come see me when he gets well."

That was the beginning of the Major's interest in Eneas. He had decided that day that he would help the boy in any way possible, because he was a boy of quality. You would be shirking your duty if you failed to recognize and to help a boy of his sort. The only question was, how to help?

When he saw the boy again, some weeks later, his mind saw the problem clearly. "Eneas," he said, "I'm going to help you. I'll see that the old folks are taken care of, so you won't have to think about them. Maybe the old man won't have rheumatism next year, anyhow. If he does, I'll find a family where he and the old lady can move in and be looked after. Don't worry about them. Just think about yourself and what I'm going to do for you. Eneas, when it comes school time, I'm going to send you away. How do you like that?" The Major smiled at his own happy idea.

There was silence. No shy smiling, no look of gratitude, only silence. Probably he had not understood.

"You understand, Eneas? Your grandparents will be taken care of. You'll go away and learn things. You'll go on a train."

The boy looked here and there and scratched at the ground with his foot. "Why do I have to go away?"

"You don't have to, Eneas. Nobody will make you. I thought you'd like to. I thought—" The Major paused, confused.

"You won't make me go away, will you?" There was fear in the voice, tears threatened.

"Why, no Eneas. If you don't want to go. I thought—"

The Major dropped the subject. He didn't see the boy again through spring and summer, but he thought of him. In fact, he couldn't forget the picture he had of him that first day. He couldn't forget either that he wanted to help him. Whether the boy understood what was good for him or not, he meant to see to it that the right thing was done. And that was why, when he made up a quota

of children to be sent to the school in Oregon, the name of Eneas
Lamartine was included. The Major did not discuss it with him
again but he set the wheels in motion. The boy would go with the
others. In time to come, he would understand. Possibly he would
be grateful.

Thirty children were included in the quota, and of them all Eneas
was the only one the Major had actual knowledge of, the only one
in whom he was personally interested. With each of them, it was
true, he had had difficulties. None had wanted to go. They said
they "liked it at home," or they were "afraid" to go away, or they
would "get sick" in a strange country; and the parents were no help.
They too were frightened and uneasy. It was a tiresome, hard kind
of duty, but the Major knew what was required of him and never
hesitated. The difference was, that in the cases of all these others,
the problem was routine. He met it, and passed over it. But in the
case of Eneas, he was bothered. He wanted to make clear what this
moment of going away meant. It was a breaking away from fear and
doubt and ignorance. Here began the new. Mark it, remember it.

His eyes lingered on Eneas. There he stood, drooping, his nose
running as on that first day, his stockings coming down, his jacket
in need of buttons. But under that shabbiness, the Major knew, was
real quality. There was a boy who, with the right help, would blossom and grow strong. It was important that he should not go away
hurt and resentful.

The Major called back his straying thoughts and cleared his
throat. The moment was important.

"Boys and girls—"

The train was pounding near. Already it had emerged from
the canyon and momently the headlong flying locomotive loomed
blacker and larger. A white plume flew upward—*Whoo-oo, whoo-oo.*

The Major realized in sudden sharp remorse that he had waited
too long. The vital moment had come, and he had paused, looked
for words, and lost it. The roar of rolling steel was upon them.

Lifting his voice in desperate haste, his eyes fastened on Eneas,
he bellowed: "Boys and girls—be good—"

That was all anyone heard.

Hard Riding

D'ARCY MCNICKLE

Riding his gray mare a hard gallop in the summer dust, Brinder Mather labored with thought which couldn't quite come into focus.

The horse labored too, its gait growing heavy as loose sand fouled its footing; but at each attempt to break stride into a trot there was the prick of spur point, a jerk at the reins. It was a habit with the rider.

"Keep going! Earn your feed, you hammerhead!"—

Brinder was always saying that his horses didn't earn their feed, yet he was the hardest rider in the country.

Feeling as he did about horses, he quite naturally had doubts about Indians. And he had to work with Indians. He was their super-intendent—a nurse to their helplessness was the way he sometimes thought of it.

It was getting toward sundown. The eastward mirror of the sky reflected orange and crimson flame thwarting the prismatic heavens. It was after supper, after a hardy day at the Agency office, and Brinder was anxious to get his task done and be home to rest. The heat of the day had fagged him. His focusing thought came out in words, audibly.

"They've been fooling with the idea for a month, more than a month, and I still can't tell what they'll do. Somehow I've got to pull it over. Either put it over or drop it. I'll tell them that. Take it or leave it. . . ."

Ahead, another mile, he saw the white schoolhouse, the windows ablaze with the evening sun. He wondered if those he had called together would be there, if they would all be there. A full turn-out, he reasoned, would indicate that they were interested. He could be encouraged if he saw them all on hand.

As he drew nearer he observed that a group stood waiting. He tried to estimate the number—twelve [or] fifteen. Others were still coming. There were riders in the distance coming by other roads. The frown relaxed on his heavy, sun-reddened face. For the moment he was satisfied. He had called the entire Tribal Council of twenty, and evidently they would all be on hand. Good!

He let his horse slow to less than a canter for the first time in the three-mile ride from the agency.

"Hello, boys. Everybody coming tonight? Let's go inside."

He strode, tall and dignified, through the group.

They smiled to his words, saying nothing. One by one they followed him into the schoolroom. He was always for starting things with a rush; they always hung back. It was a familiar pattern. He walked to the teacher's desk and spread out before him a sheaf of paper which he had brought in a heavy envelope.

In five years one got to know something about Indians. Even in one's first job as superintendent of a reservation, five years was a good schooling.

The important thing, the first thing to learn, was not to let them stall you. They would do it every time if you let them. They would say to a new idea, "Let us talk about that," or "Give us time. We'll think about it." One had to know when to cut short. Put it over or drop it. Take it or leave it.

Not realizing that at the start, he had let these crazy mountain Indians stall on him a long time before he had begun to get results. He had come to them with a simple idea and only now, after five years, was it beginning to work.

Cattle—that was the idea. Beef cattle. Blooded stock. Good bulls. Fall round-ups. The shipment east. Cash profits. In language as simple as that he had finally got them to see his point. He had a special liking for cattle. It began long before he had ever seen an Indian, back home in New York State. Boyhood reading about hard riding and fast shooting on the cattle trails—that was what started it. Then, in his first job in the Indian Service, he had worked under a hard-minded Scotchman whose record as a stockman was unbeatable. He had learned the gospel from him. He learned to talk the lingo.

"Indians don't know, more than that don't give a damn, about dragging their feet behind a plow. Don't say as I blame 'em. But Indians'll always ride horses. They're born to that. And if they're going to ride horses, they might as well be riding herd on a bunch of steers. It pays money."

He put it that way, following his Scotch preceptor. He put it to the Indians, to Washington officials, and to anybody he could buttonhole for a few minutes. It was a complete gospel. It was appropriations of money from Congress for cattle purchases. It won flattering remarks from certain interested visitors who were always around inquiring about Indian welfare. In time, it won over the Indians. It should have won them sooner.

The point was just that, not to let them stall on you. After five years he had learned his lesson. Put it over, or drop it.

He had taken off his broad-brimmed cattleman's hat and laid it on the desk beside his papers. The hat was part of the creed. He surveyed the score of wordless, pensive, buckskin-smelling Indians, some slouched forward, holding their big hats between their knees; others, hats on, silently smoking.

He had to put it across, this thing he wanted them to do. He had to do it now, tonight, or else drop it. That was what he had concluded.

"I think you fellows have learned a lot since I been with you. I appreciate the way you co-operate with me. Sometimes it's kinda hard to make things clear, but once you see what it means to you, you're all for it. I like that." He paused and mopped his brow. The schoolroom was an oven. The meeting should have been held outside— but never mind.

"In our stock association, we run out cattle together on a common range. We share the costs of riding range, rounding up, branding, and buying breeding bulls. Every time you sell a steer you pay a five-dollar fee into the pot, and that's what pays the bills. That's one of the things I had to tell you about. You didn't understand at first, but once you did, you went ahead. Today, it's paying dividends.

"You never had as much cash profit in your life before. Your steers are better beef animals, because the breeding is better. We got the class in bulls. And you get better prices because you can dicker with the buyers. But you all know that. I'm just reminding you."

Someone coughed in the back of the room, and Brinder, always on guard, like the cowboys contending with rustlers and sheepmen he used to read about, straightened his back and looked sharply. But it was only a cough, repeated several times—an irritating, ineffective kind of cigarette cough. No one else in the audience made a sound. All were held in the spell of Brinder's words, or at any rate were waiting for him to finish what he had to say.

"We have one bad defect yet. You know what I mean, but I'll mention it just the same. In other words, fellows, we all of us know that every year a certain number of cattle disappear. The wolves don't get them, and they don't die of natural causes. They are always strong, fat, two- or three-year-old steers that disappear, the kind that wolves don't monkey with and that don't die naturally. I ain't pointing my finger at anybody, but you know as well as I do that there's a certain element on the Reservation that don't deserve fresh meat but always has it. They're too lazy or too ornery or they just don't know what it's all about. But they get fresh meat just the same.

"I want you fellows to get this. Let it sink in deep. Every time a fat steer goes to feed some Slick Steve too lazy to earn his keep, some of you are out around seventy-five, eighty dollars. You lose that much. Ponder that, you fellows."

He rustled papers on the desk, looking for a row of figures: number of beef animals lost in five years (estimated), their money value, in round numbers. He hurled his figures at them, cudgeling.

"Some of you don't mind the loss, because it's poor people getting the meat. It keeps somebody from starving. That's what you say. What I say is—that ain't a proper way to look at it. First of all, because it's stealing, and we can't go to countenancing stealing, putting up with it, I mean. Nobody has to starve, remember that. If you want to do something on your own hook for the old people who can't work, you can. You can do what you like with your money. But lazy people, these Slick Steves who wouldn't work on a bet, nobody should give it easy to them, that's what I'm saying."

He waited a moment, letting the words find their way home. "There's a solution, as I told you last month. We want to set up a

court, a court of Indian judges, and you will deal with these fellows
in your own way. Give a few of them six months in jail to think it
over, and times will begin to change around here . . ."

That was the very point he had reached the last time he talked
to the Council, a month before. He had gone no further, then, because they had begun to ask questions, and from their questions he
had discovered that they hadn't the least idea what he was driving
at. Or so they made it appear. "If we have a tribal court," somebody
would ask, "do we have to put somebody in jail?" That, obviously,
was intentionally naive. It was intended to stall him off. Or some
old man would say, "If somebody has to go to jail, let the Superintendent do it. Why should we have to start putting our own people
in jail?" Such nonsense as that had been talked.

Finally, the perennial question of money came up. Would the
Government pay for the court? A treacherous question, and he had
answered without flinching.

"That's another thing," he had said brightly. "We're going to
get away from the idea of the Government paying for everything.
Having your own business this way, making a profit from it, you can
pay for this yourselves. That will make you independent. It will be
your own court, not the Government's court, not the Superintendent's court. No, the court will be supported by the fee money you
pay when you sell a steer."

That speech broke up the meeting. It was greeted by a confusion
of talk in the native tongue which gradually subsided in favor of one
speaker, one of the ancients, who obviously was a respected leader.
Afterwards, a young English-speaking tribesman translated.

"The old man here, Looking Glass, says the Gover'ment don't
give us nothing for nothing. The money it spends on us, that's our
own money, he says. It belongs to us and they keep it there at Washington, and nobody can say how much it is or how much has been
lost. He says, Where is all that money that they can't afford to pay
for this court? That's what he says."

There was the snare which tripped up most Agency plans, scratch
an old Indian and the reaction was always the same. "Where's the
money the Government owes us? Where's our land? Where's our
treaty?" They were like a whistle with only one stop, those old fel-

lows. Their tune was invariable, relentless, and shrill. That was why one dreaded holding a meeting when the old men were present. Now the young fellows, who understood Agency plans . . .

Anyhow, here he was trying it again, going over the plan with great care and patience. Much of the misunderstanding had been ironed out in the meantime. So he had been led to believe.

"This court will put an end to all this trouble," he was going on, trying to gauge the effect of his words, watching for a reaction. At last it came. One of the old men was getting to his feet.

He was a small man, emaciated by age and thin living, yet neat looking. His old wife obviously took good care of his clothes, sewed buckskin patches on his overalls and kept him in new moccasins. He talked firmly yet softly, and not for very long. He sat down as soon as he had finished and let the interpreter translate for him.

"The old man here, Big Face, says the court maybe is all right. They have talked it over among themselves, and maybe it's all right. Our agent, he says, is a good man. He rides too fast. He talks too fast. But he has a good heart, so maybe the court is all right. That's what Big Face say."

The words were good, and Brinder caught himself smiling, which was bad practice when dealing with the old fellows. They were masters at laying traps for the unwary—that, too, he had learned in five years. Their own expressions never changed, once they got going, and you could never tell what might be in their minds.

Just the same, he felt easier. Big Face, the most argumentative of the lot, had come around to accepting this new idea, and that was something gained. The month had not been lost.

Big Face had something more to say. He was getting to his feet again, giving a tug to his belt and looking around, as if to make sure of his following. He had been appointed spokesman. That much was clear.

He made a somewhat longer speech in which he seemed to express agitation, perhaps uncertainty. One could never be sure of tone values. Sometimes the most excitable-sounding passages of this strange tongue were very tame in English. Brinder had stopped smiling and waited for the translation.

"Big Face, here, says there's only one thing they can't decide about. That's about judges. Nobody wants to be a judge. That's what they don't like. Maybe the court is all right, but nobody wants to be judge."

Brinder was rather stumped by that. He rose to his feet quickly, giving everyone a sharp glance. Was this a trap?

"Tell the old man I don't understand that. It is an honor being a judge. People pay to be a judge in some places. Tell Big Face I don't understand his objection."

The old man was on his feet as soon as the words had been translated for him.

"It's like this. To be a judge, you got to be about perfect. You got to know everything, and you got to live up to it. Otherwise, you got nothing to say to anybody who does wrong. Anybody who puts himself up to be that good, he's just a liar. And people will laugh at him. We are friends among ourselves, and nobody interferes in another person's business. That's how it is, and nobody wants to set himself up to be a judge. That's what Big Face says."

There it was, as neatly contrived a little pitfall as he had ever seen. He had to admire it—all the time letting himself get furious. Not that he let them see it. No, in five years he had learned that much. Keep your head, and when in doubt, talk your head off. He drew a deep breath and plunged into an explanation of all the things he had already explained, reminding them of the money they lost each year, of the worthless fellows who were making an easy living from their efforts, and of the proper way to deal with the problem. He repeated all the arguments and threw in as many more as he could think of.

"You have decided all this. You agree the court is a good thing. But how can you have a court without judges? It's the judges that make a court."

He couldn't tell whether he was getting anywhere or not—in all likelihood, not. They were talking all together once more, and it didn't look as if they were paying much attention to him. He waited.

"What's it all about?" he finally asked the interpreter, a young mixed-blood, who was usually pretty good about telling Brinder which way the wind of thought blew among the old people.

"I can't make out," the interpreter murmured, drawing closer to

Brinder. "They are saying lots of things. But I think they're going to decide on the judges—they've got some kind of plan—watch out for it—now, one of the old men will speak."

It was Big Face rising to his feet once more. Looking smaller, more wizened than ever. The blurring twilight of the room absorbed some of his substance and made Brinder feel that he was losing his grip on the situation. A shadow is a difficult adversary, and Big Face was rapidly turning into one.

"The Agent wants this court. He thinks it's a good thing. So we have talked some more, and we agree. We will have this court." He paused briefly, allowing Brinder only a moment's bewilderment.

"Only we couldn't decide who would be judge. Some said this one, some said that one. It was hard . . ."

Brinder coughed. "Have you decided on anyone, Big Face?" He no longer knew which way things were drifting but hoped for the best.

The old fellow's eyes, misted by age, actually twinkled. In the body of councillors, somebody laughed and coughed in the same breath. Feet stirred and bodies shifted. Something was in the air. Haltingly, Big Face named the men—the most amazing trio the Reservation had to offer.

"Walks-in-the-Ground, Jacob Gopher, Twisted Horn."

In the silence that followed, Brinder tried hard to believe he had heard the wrong names. A mistake had been made. It was impossible to take it seriously. These three men—no, it was impossible! The first, an aged imbecile dripping saliva—ready to die! The second, stone deaf and blind! The third, an utter fool, a half-witted clown, to whom no one listened.

"You mean this?" Brinder still could not see the full situation, but was afraid that the strategy was deliberate and final.

"These will be the judges of this court," Big Face replied, smiling in his usual friendly way.

"But these men can't be judges! They are too old, or else too foolish. No one will listen to them—" Brinder broke off short. He saw that he had stated the strategy of the old men especially as they had intended it. His friendliness withered away.

Big Face did not hesitate, did not break off smiling. "It is better, we think, that fools should be judges. If people won't listen to them, no one will mind."

Brinder had nothing to say, not just then. He let the front legs of his chair drop to the floor, picked up his hat. His face had paled. After five years, still to let this happen. Using great effort, he turned it off as a joke. "Boys, you should of elected me judge to your kangaroo court. I would have made a crackerjack."

The Indians just laughed and didn't know what he meant, not exactly. But maybe he was right.

ABOUT THE EDITOR

Bernd Peyer is a Swiss citizen who was reared in South America and educated in the United States. He received his doctorate in American Studies from the Johann Wolfgang Goethe Universität in Frankfurt in 1978, and since then he has been a lecturer in the department of ethnology there. He has published a number of articles on American Indian literature and with Peter Bolz co-authored a book on American Indian art entitled *Indianische Kunst Nordamerikas*.